FUNNY GIRL

FUNNY GIRL

GIRL

Funniest. Stories.
EVER.

Edited by **BETSY BIRD**

Viking

Viking

An imprint of Penguin Random House LLC

375 Hudson Street

New York, New York 10014

First published in the United States of America by Viking,
an imprint of Penguin Random House LLC, 2017

LIBRARY OF CONGRESS CATALOGING-IN-PUBLICATION DATA IS AVAILABLE

ISBN 9780451477316

Printed in U.S.A.

1 3 5 7 9 10 8 6 4 2

Set in Eames Century Modern
Book design by Nancy Brennan

For Lillian. The original funny girl.

Contents

Introduction xi

by Betsy Bird

How to Tell a Joke 1

by Delaney Yeager and Mackenzie Yeager

In Which Young Raina Learns a Lesson 9

by Raina Telgemeier

Dear Grandpa: Give Me Money 14

by Alison DeCamp

Grandma in Oil Country: A True Story 29

by Ursula Vernon

One Hot Mess 43

by Carmen Agra Deedy

Fleamail 52

by Deborah Underwood

A Most Serious Recitation of the Poem "Trees" 61

by Cece Bell

Things Could Be Verse 68
by Kelly DiPucchio

Swimming Is for Other Kids 72
by Akilah Hughes

Dear Bella and Rover 78
by Deborah Underwood

The Thumb Incident 80
by Meghan McCarthy

Desdemona and Sparks Go All In 90
by Rita Williams-Garcia and Michelle Garcia

7 Things I Thought Were (Think Are) Funny
but Were Really Kind of Sad, and That All Happened
to My Little Brother 100
by Lisa Brown

Babysitting Nightmare 102
by Shannon Hale

Dear Bella and Rover (Again) 112
by Deborah Underwood

Can We Talk About Whiskers? 114
by Jennifer L. Holm, art by Matthew Holm

Brown Girl Pop Quiz: All of the Above. 121
by Mitali Perkins

Over and Out. 128
by Lisa Graff

Doodle 140
by Amy Ignatow

Fleamail Pawed-cast 143
by Deborah Underwood

How to Play Imaginary Games 146
by Leila Sales

Great Expectations 150
by Christine Mari Inzer

A Public Service Announcement About Your Period
from Sarah T. Wrigley, Age 12¾ 154
by Libba Bray

The Smart Girl's Guide to the Chinese Zodiac 161
by Lenore Look

Bad Luck Dress 176
by Charise Mericle Harper

The World's Most Awkward Mermaid 179
by Sophie Blackall

Tell Your Future with Mad Libs® 185

My Life Being Funny
(and How You Can Do It, Too) 188
by Adrianne Chalepah

About the Contributors 195

Introduction

By Betsy Bird

Once upon a time, I got my superpowers confused.

When I was in middle school, I was convinced that I was basically an invisible ninja. I seemed to have the otherworldly power to not get noticed by anyone, ever. Here, I'll give you an example. See this picture?

Okay. Now, did you notice how your eyes just slid across the page to get away from it? THAT WAS MY POWER! And it was awesome. With this ability I was able to slink through seventh grade without anyone noticing that they should make fun of me. Even teachers barely saw me. Bullies would target me for one second and then, like butter falling off a cob of corn, they'd move on to someone else. I was the queen of Invisibilia.

Until I wasn't.

That's the lesson of all stories of invisibility, isn't it? You start to get cocky. You start thinking you can get away with stuff. And the thing I wanted to get away with was staring at boys.

In this particular case the object of my affection was an older man (an eighth grader) named Andrew Seidel. Here's what I knew about him:

1) He read *National Geographic* for fun.

This was, to me, the height of sophistication, so I silently adored him from afar. And I would have gotten away with my creepy stalking if, for some reason, my cloak of invisibility hadn't slipped off when I wasn't looking.

One day I was going to shop class, and there was Andrew walking ahead of me. Excellent. I was an

Olympian when it came to back-of-the-head staring. But then all of a sudden he turned around, and walked right at me. Not by me. *At* me. He stopped, looked me dead in the eye, and said quite clearly, "Look, I know who you are, okay? *I know who you are.*"

First off, that was the last thing I expected to hear coming out of Andrew Seidel's mouth. Second, I wasn't entirely certain it was true. What he must have meant was that he knew I was staring at him like a freak all the time. I bet he'd received some advice from his mom on how to deal with me. "Just tell her you know she exists, honey. That's all she wants."

There are a lot of things I could have said or done in that moment. But what my brain elected to do was this: *I acted like he was the psycho one.*

I looked at the guy, raised one eyebrow (eyebrow raising was one of the only marketable talents that I knew I had), and said in a voice dripping with distaste, "Uh . . . *okay.* . . ." And I backed away slowly like he was a rabid dog. Then I turned and walked into shop class, where I puzzled over what had just happened.

The question before me was this: Was I or was I not a husk of my former self, now destroyed with embarrassment? Because here's the thing: I could have been. The object of my affection had just come within a hairsbreadth of getting a restraining order against me.

That's not good. I should, by rights, have been mortified, begging the nearest handsaw to come and put me out of my miserable existence immediately.

But ... but ... it was just so funny!

I mean, come on. You have to admit it. I knew that according to all the magazines and stuff I heard, I was now supposed to be flailing on the floor, berating myself. My self-esteem, by all logic, was meant to plummet. I was supposed to care deeply what other people thought of me, and I did (sorta kinda), but it's hard to be down on yourself when you find yourself funny. Or when you find the kernel of humor in dire situations.

Thanks to Andrew Seidel (who sort of disappears from my memory after that point), I figured out who I was that day. I'm *not* actually invisible. People see me, and that can sometimes be good and sometimes be bad. But I discovered my true superpower that day:

I have a sense of humor.

Let's say something wacky happens to you. Like, your mom sets the bathtub on fire in front of a crowd of possible new friends. Or you take a swim test in your clothes and nearly drown. Let's say you go to a party and accidentally flash your entire class. Are you gonna cry about this and carry it to your grave? Are you gonna give that moment power over you? Or are you going to decide that it's funny, and own it?

I choose the latter, and so do all the authors in this book. Every single person contributing to *Funny Girl* (with the exception of one little brother) was a girl once. And now they're funny women. Amazing, fantastic, funny women. Some of them you may already be familiar with. Others will be new to you. But all of them know that a sense of humor is the best superpower you can have. And guess what? It can be *your* superpower, too.

FUNNY GIRL

How to Tell a Joke

By Delaney Yeager and Mackenzie Yeager

A couple of wise women once said, "Joke-telling is the greatest superpower a gal can possess." Those wise women were us. Just now. While writing this. And you know what? We were right. Nay, *are* right. The ability to tell a joke is a great superpower. Some are born with a good sense of humor (just as some are born incredible forklift operators), but being able to deliver a joke isn't something you're *just* born with. It takes know-how and lots of practice . . . complete with failures, weird glances, and cricket noises. But we're here to help!

Before we get into the thick of it, you need to know the one hard-and-fast rule in joke-telling: *confidence.* You're funny! Your best friend knows it! Your family knows it! *You* know it! Telling a joke is a way of "putting yourself out there," and that can feel kinda scary and risky. But do you know what helps those feelings?

Selling it, baby! Telling a joke with confidence is what it's all about.

Now, let's learn . . .

HOW!

TO!

TELL!

A!

JOKE!

How to Tell a Joke . . . at the Dinner Table:

The dinner table at home is a great place to start. There is very little risk involved because everyone there already thinks you're the coolest. Bonus: food is funny. (For proof, type "Charlie Chaplin dinner roll dance" into YouTube. Also, *Pee-Wee's Big Adventure* breakfast.") And, if you choose the right moment, your dinner table joke could become a family legend.

A DELANEY STORY: One night my dad had worked tirelessly to make tuna noodle casserole, a meal I had never seen or tried before. It's a funky-looking dish: picture a cooked lasagna with noodles and tuna salad. Sounds disgusting, right? It's dee-LISH. Anyway, Dad calls us all down for dinner. The family and I are sitting around the table, and he brings out the casserole. Before he can tell us what it is, six-year-old me pipes up with, "What're we having for dinner? Vomit?" Everyone laughed, and it's referenced at family dinners TO THIS VERY DAY!

That wasn't the greatest joke ever told, but everyone in the room cracked up! Here's why: timing, observation, and surprise.

Timing: Our dad had just presented this dish, meaning everyone's attention was on the meal. We were all looking at the same thing. Perfect moment for a joke!

Observation: That thing looked gross! Like unidentified cafeteria mush trying to disguise itself as something normal, but failing. And let's not pretend that the smell of cooked fish wafting through the house is very charming either. So, I compared the foreign dish to something I was much more familiar with: puke.

Surprise: Our dad had worked hard preparing this dish. Everyone was probably expecting a comment more like "Oh, this looks scrumptious! Thank you, Father dear!" or "Ooh la la, look how fancy and casserole-y!" But instead, I surprised the room with an opposite reaction. These three techniques can be used in joke-telling anytime, anywhere!

How to Tell a Joke . . . in the Classroom:

The classroom—though slightly trickier than the dinner table—is a perfect joke-telling setting. But be warned, you want to be seen as funny, not the "class clown." You know that kid we're talking about: yells, bothers the teacher, tries too hard to get attention? While people may laugh at this kid's jokes, you do not want to be this kid. This kid generally has VB (visible boogers).

A MACKENZIE STORY: One fateful day in third grade, my school was having an assembly on not doing drugs (as you do), and the speaker had a Luke Skywalker–esque robot hand. This wasn't revealed until the climax of his story, when he yelled "I WAS ON DRUGS AND THE NEXT DAY I WOKE UP IN A DITCH WITH MY HAND CUT OFF!" And then, to prove to us he wasn't lying, he rotated his robot hand all the way around, and everyone screamed because it was terrifying. (Or because some kids weren't paying attention and were like, "Hey, Peter, want to play Magic cards after schoo—AHHH WHAT IS THAT GUY'S HAND DOING?!? I KNEW A ROBOT INVASION WAS UPON US!!!")

About a month later, I had to give a report to my class on robotics or technology or something I was vaguely terrible at. At the end of the presentation, without mentioning the former drug addict guy, I rotated a fake hand I was holding underneath my sleeve. Everyone laughed because it was a simple reference to a shared experience most had forgotten. At the time, I didn't know this had a name or a firm place in joke history. Funny girls, I introduce you to "the callback"—when you make a joke that connects with something that happened a while ago. The callback, much like a baby spooked by the sound of its own fart, is almost always funny.

How to Tell a Joke . . .
in Class When Reading Aloud:

There's nothing worse than having to listen to someone read aloud in class when they are monotone, quiet, and petrified. So when it's your turn, get into it. (I mean, don't go overboard and come in dressed like Sarah, Plain and Tall. Unless you want to.) Try doing voices, mouth-based sound effects, or reading lines that end with an exclamation point in an EXCLAMATORY WAY, LIKE THIS!

If you're thinking, "Okay, I did it a little bit, but if I keep this voice going, people will get bored of it," you're wrong! They love it! They want more! Your commitment to your reading will perk people up, make them laugh, and get them into the book. Added bonus: your teacher will like you more for being enthusiastic. Check-plus in participation, here you come!

How to Tell a Joke . . . at Play Rehearsal:

Take an object, and . . . wait for it . . . use it in a way it's not generally used! Boom. This is called "prop humor." Let's say you're playing the lovable yet rapacious orphan Pepper in *Annie*. Take your orphan broom, put it through the arm of your T-shirt (or dirty orphan smock, if you're in dress rehearsals), and pretend to have a wooden arm.

Now be an old sea dog! Or spin it around and scream, "I WAS ON DRUGS AND I WOKE UP IN A DITCH WITH MY HAND CUT OFF!" . . . Actually that one might not play in this situation. Stick with "sea dog."

Some of you may be thinking, "That sounds really stupid." And you are correct. It is really stupid. But a lot of times, the sheer moronic nature of something is why people laugh. Remember! If you do something with confidence, it generally won't fail. Plus, you're a bored orphan in musical rehearsal, just tryin' to get by, so it's okay.

Now go out there and play with those props that you're not supposed to be playing with!

How to Tell a Joke . . . at a Birthday Party:

Birthday parties are the best place to make grown-ups laugh. And it feels really good to make old people laugh. It's like giving to charity, or something. Because old people's lives are full of sad, monotonous things like paying taxes, and watching the news, and making sure their automatic e-mail signatures look professional. Plus, they're probably stressed, as they've been working so hard to put this party together. They need a good chuckle.

There is a very easy formula for this: pretend like it isn't a party for kids. Say and do things your parents would say and do at a grown-up party. For example, when a mom or dad asks what you'd like to drink, say the name of the drink you want, then say "on the rocks." Like, "Coca-Cola, on the rocks." Or, if you don't like ice in your drink, say "Coca-Cola, neat." This is a joke for parents. They'll like it, they'll laugh really hard, and then they'll go tell the other parents about it. And all your friends will be like, "Duhhhh, what does that even mean?" And you'll get to roll your eyes and be like, "Nothing. It's just for the adults. Go back to your game of tag, plebes."

Another example: Say there's a bouncy house, or some other high-energy activity. A great line while you take a break is, "I'm getting too old for this." Or something about how brittle and old your bones are. Maybe mention your hip problems. The grown-ups will laugh because you are being "ironic," while also making them feel understood.

How to Tell a Joke . . .
When Dealing with a Bully:

If someone's being mean to you, don't be mean right back at them. Not only is that too easy, but it's what your bully *wants* you to do. Instead, do something they will never expect: make jokes! If a bully makes fun of something you're wearing, a great way to shut them up is to join in. Have a solid joke prepared about your own outfit, and be ready to say it when that dumb bully gives you an opportunity.

For example: say you're rockin' a super-fine pair o' overalls (which are so back in, and these two writers are so happy about it). Now, because mean girls wear boring clothes, one might look you up and down and sneer and go, "What are you wearing?" That's when you respond, in a cartoonishly heavy Southern accent, "M' farm clothes!" and walk away. You'll have made a few onlookers laugh, and the mean girl will be totally thrown off, which means you win.

* * *

In conclusion, just go for it. There will be times when people make you feel like you're not funny, you can't be funny, or you *shouldn't* be funny, just because you're a girl. Some boys are intimidated by funny girls. Or some girls who think that being popular or blending in is the most important thing in the world can also feel threatened or confused by your sense of humor. When people respond that way, remember that they're wrong, and then prove it to them with your own brand of funny. Then go home and read this book written by women who have faced this same thing all their lives.

Now . . . make a fart noise with your mouth, because this paragraph was way too serious.

THE END!

In Which Young Raina Learns a Lesson

By Raina Telgemeier

Dear Grandpa: Give Me Money

By Alison DeCamp

Dear Grandpa,

I need some money. Now. I have enclosed an envelope for your convenience.
    Make it a lot of money.

> Love,
> Delilah (aka Trixie)

* * *

Dear Trixie,

First of all, never, ever, EVER use Comic Sans. It's a horrible font used only by ax murderers and people who think acrostic poems are actual poetry.
    Secondly, Trixie, I refuse to indulge this need to change your name on a daily basis—half the time I can't remember your name as it is. Let's not make it harder.

Thirdly, I would like someone to give me large amounts of money as well. I would also like world peace, the winning lottery numbers, tickets to the Women's World Cup, and a drone to use with my GoPro—hooking it up to the dog's collar just isn't cutting it anymore. How many times can I watch Mr. Pickles lick himself?

I will, however, give you a dollar if you come clean Cupcake's litter box.

Love,

Grandpa

* * *

Dear Grandpa,

In case you couldn't see my earlier request, I will now write it in larger letters. I hear old people sometimes can't see very well.

I need money! It's urgent!

Also, I don't clean litter boxes for anything less than $15 per hour. Or if Mom makes me.

Love,

' Tabitha (aka Trixie)

* * *

Dear Trixie,

Papyrus is almost as bad as Comic Sans. It's a font used only by kidnappers and people who think French fries are really French.

    Also, I don't have any money. I live on social security, canned mac and cheese, and air. Go bug someone else.

I love you,
Grandpa

*   *   *

Dear Grandpa,

I have it on good authority (meaning Mom told me) that you went out with that gold digger, Margaret Baker, four times last week. (Mom's words, not mine. I'm not judging that gold digger at all.) So, apparently, there's a bit more money there than you're letting on.

    I hate for it to come to this, but I'm enclosing a picture to let you know just what might happen if my request for a monetary donation is not met.

I love you, too.
Ariana (aka Trixie)

*   *   *

Dear Trixie,

What, in the name of all that is holy, is this font you used? It's burning my eyes! I can't see! I'm melting!

I'm not kidding. That lettering is so bad I showed it to the cat and she threw up a hair ball. Don't worry; I won't make you come clean it up. The dog already ate it.

Now, please ask your mother to mind her own beeswax. And, for your information (and which you might want to share with your mother), Margaret Baker happens to be a former nun. And a corporate attorney with offices in San Francisco and New York. Truth be told, I might be the gold digger in this relationship.

The picture you sent appears to be cut from the antique book I gave you last Christmas. Are you threatening to hug Cupcake if I don't give you money? Remember the last time you hugged her? I think the scratches are still faintly visible, if I'm not mistaken.

What's with the letter writing? Shouldn't we be texting like we usually do? Or Snapchatting? What's the point of my Apple Watch if I can't use it?

hmu,
Grandpa

*   *   *

DEAR GRANDPA,

MOM TOOK MY PHONE AND CHANGED THE WI-FI PASSWORD RIGHT AFTER SHE FOUND MY "HOW TO FORCE PEOPLE TO GIVE YOU MONEY" SEARCH LAST WEEK. BELIEVE ME, I WOULD MUCH RATHER BE TEXTING YOU—I'M PRETTY SURE MY THUMBS HAVE BEEN GETTING WEAKER, AND I'M TIRED OF RUNNING UP AND DOWN

THE STAIRS TO SLIDE THESE LETTERS UNDER YOUR DOOR.

DO YOU HAVE MY MONEY?

LOVE,

DANIELLA (AKA TRIXIE)

*   *   *

Dear Trixie,

I feel like your last letter a) was yelling at me (never use ALL CAPS!), and b) should have been chiseled in stone and discovered by archaeologists at some Roman ruins. You must become more responsible in your font choices, or I can't be held responsible for my actions.

I am lol-ing because you got in trouble with your parents. LOL. LOL. ROTFL.

Now, why exactly are you so desperate for money?

Love,

Grandpa

*   *   *

Dear Grandpa,

I picked this lettering just for you! Because I am thoughtful that way.

Remember our neighbor Carmela? Well, she always has the newest everything—shoes, phones, clothes, dogs, you name it. She is very popular, and I want to be her best friend. In order to be her best friend, I have to have the newest everything, too. If I were her best friend, I would be happy for the rest of my life.

I need money to buy the newest everything and be happy for the rest of my life.

Hand it over, old guy.

You're my favorite grandpa.
Hazel (aka Trixie)

*   *   *

Dear Trixie,

That lettering makes me dizzy. Obviously you care nothing about my health or you wouldn't subject me to such torture.

Also, here's a little hint from the old guy: money can't buy you happiness. It's true it can buy you sea salt caramel ice cream with chocolate sprinkles, and that is really close to happiness. But in the grand scheme of things, ice cream melts and people who only like you for what you have (and not who you are) are worse than melted ice cream. They are the ice cream that falls off the cone before you even have a chance to lick it.

Whatever happened to the little girl who liked digging in the mud for worms and then refused to take a bath for fear the bacteria on her body would die—washed down the drain like their little microscopic lives didn't even matter? I liked her. She was cute.

Please find that girl and return her unharmed in a brown, unmarked paper bag. Do not involve the cops.

Love,

Grandpa

* * *

Dear Grandpa,

You've been watching Law & Order again, haven't you? Didn't Mom ask you to stop? Remember when you kept running around the neighborhood arresting people? That was totally embarrassing. Please don't make us put you in a home.

I won't tell Mom about your senile Law & Order addiction if you promptly deliver the money I have so patiently been waiting for.

Patiently waiting,
Gloria (aka Trixie)

*   *   *

Dear Trixie,

Your last letter was a bit worrisome. Was that real blood you used to write it? I hope so, because otherwise it loses a lot of its scariness.

    Oh, let's face it. You aren't scaring me. Go ahead and put me in a home. The food has got to be better than the mush you keep giving me. What was that you made for lunch? Gruel? Porridge mixed with slugs? And did you add some dark chocolate?

    Very fancy!

Still hungry,
Grandpa (aka Grandpa)

*   *   *

Dear Grandpa (if you are who you say you are),

That was spaghetti! I spent 45 minutes boiling those noodles. Sure, they might have been a little stuck together, but in Italy that's how they like them. I know this because my friend Juan said that was true. I then warmed up the sauce in the microwave and combined the ingredients into a spectacular feast. I can't help it if your taste buds have all died.

And I might have added some Nutella. Accidentally.

I was eating a little snack.

I must admit you have hurt my feelings, but I will pretend this little misunderstanding never happened if you give me $$$.

Still broke,
Charlotte (aka Trixie)

*   *   *

Dear Trixie,

You will never, ever have enough money to be Carmela's friend. A friend will like you no matter what. Look at me. I'm your friend, and you have never given me anything but a headache.

Me. Waiting for you to realize I won't be giving you any money.

I'm attaching a picture. I cut it out just for you. It's like Snapchatting, except it doesn't disappear in ten seconds. So it's more like Slowchatting. Hmm . . . I should probably trademark that.

Love,
Grandpa

*   *   *

Dear Grandpa,

How can you so easily forget all of your failed inventions? I'm afraid to tell you that "Slowchatting" is one of your worst ideas yet. People ain't got no time for that. We are busy.

Also, I couldn't read whatever you wrote on that picture. I tried, but I got bored halfway through.

I'm on my way to the store. Let me know if you need anything. I will need money, however. $1,000 should do the trick.

In a hurry,
Marcella (aka Trixie)

*   *   *

Dear Trixie,

You can't bamboozle me, even with your fancy letters and fancy fake name. You want to take my Slowchatting idea all for yourself and make millions. I'm no fool.

When you get to the store, would you buy more dog food? Mr. Pickles is just about out and is acting quite hangry. I fear for my life.

Love,
Grandpa

* * *

Dear Grandpa,

Here is the dog food. It was $750. I will wait outside your door for payment.

Patiently waiting,
Lucinda (aka Trixie)

* * *

Dear Trixie,

Why don't we meet in the kitchen and eat some chocolate chip cookies? I know it's almost dinner, but I won't tell if you don't.

Love,
Grandpa

* * *

Dear Grandpa,

I can't. I'm busy waiting for Carmela. She was supposed

to come over an hour ago. Do you think she was kidnapped?

Love,
Trixie

PS She's here!
PPS She has a new bike!
PPPS And a new phone!
PPPPS And maybe some new sunglasses.
PPPPPS I'm attaching an envelope for the $$$. You can see now why I need it. I'll pick it up when I get back.

* * *

Dear Trixie,

The envelope will be waiting for you when you get back.

I have filled it with a special treat.

Love,
Grandpa

* * *

Dear Grandpa,

I'm back. Thanks for the lint. Where did you get all of it, your belly button? The dryer vent? And how did you stuff so much into that little envelope? Also, why didn't you warn me about people like Carmela DeFlaco? All she cares about is money. You probably won't understand this, but money does not buy happiness.

Older and wiser, my patootie.

Sincerely yours,
Trixie

* * *

Dear Trixie,

¿Qué pasa? (That's Spanish for "'sup?")

Love,
Grandpa
(who is older and cuter—being smart is overrated)

* * *

Dear Grandpa,

What happened is I dropped the locket you and Grandma gave me. Remember the one? There's a picture of me on one side and Grandma on the other? And we look exactly alike?

I retraced my steps from the house to the park. I looked in the dirt and the drains and the grass. And then Carmela said, "It's just an old necklace. What does it matter, anyway?" Then she rode off with Nick and Margo. I sat on the curb and cried, not because I lost some friends, but because I lost my locket.

DON'T WORRY—I found it later in my shirt, tucked into my jeans.

And then I realized I'd rather eat cookies and dig up worms with you than try to be friends with people who don't know what's really important.

I hope you're writing this down because you could learn a thing or two about friendship here.

Love,
Trixie

* * *

Dear Trixie,

You bring the shovels, I'll bring the cookies. Meet you in the backyard in five.

Love,
Grandpa

Grandma in Oil Country: A True Story

By Ursula Vernon

When I was about ten years old, my grandmother decided she was going to go look at her oil land in Wyoming.

Grandma's oil land had never, to the best of our knowledge, produced any oil, but she had a certificate stating that she had inherited property in Wyoming, and she was convinced that it was only a matter of time before oil was discovered there and she became extremely rich.

Her fifth husband (who had also been her third husband—Grandma had had quite a life) decided to stay home in Oregon and play checkers. He had lost seven hundred and eighty-five games in a row, but felt that he was very close to beating the computer.

Before we left, Grandma had her hair permed. We weren't sure why. Possibly she wanted to look good when meeting her oil land for the first time.

Perms in those days were expensive and took a lot of chemicals, so it was important that she not get her hair wet for five days, or else the curls would all go flat and straight again. She was careful to pack several shower caps.

Then my mom and my grandmother and I (and our suitcases) all piled into her car and started to drive to Wyoming.

Grandma had a chocolate brown Crown Victoria, with a matching brown velour interior. It was like a couch with wheels.

We drove for almost a full ten minutes before we stopped for brunch. Grandma believed that brunch was the pinnacle of civilized behavior.

After we got back in the car, we sang songs. None of us sang very well, but this was okay because we were also all tone-deaf.

We went from Oregon through Idaho into Montana. Grandma had a road map, but she had spilled coffee over several key portions some years ago, and the route to her oil land was now a large brown blotch shaped vaguely like a chicken.

Grandma stopped at a gas station to ask for directions. Blinded by the glory of her hair, the man behind the counter asked her to marry him. She refused, so he settled for giving her directions to Wyoming.

"Take Beartooth Pass," he said. "It's the most beautiful drive in the country."

"He gave me very good directions," Grandma told us. "I bought a glass clown from him, since I couldn't marry him."

My mother sighed. Grandma put the clown in the trunk.

We followed the signs for Beartooth Pass.

The road went up and doubled back on itself, over

and over again. There were enormous mountains, and when we looked up the side of the mountain, there were tiny cars driving on roads just like ours.

LOOK AT THOSE SUCKERS! GOOD THING WE'RE NOT GOING THAT WAY.

We kept driving. The road kept going up. There were no guardrails. Grandma was a very good driver, but Crown Victorias are not good at navigating hairpin turns up a mountainside.

As we drove, the gorges got deeper and deeper.

"If you drove off the edge, you'd have time to say the Lord's Prayer before you hit the bottom," said Grandma.

GRANDMA, I THINK WE'RE ON THE ROAD THAT THOSE OTHER CARS WERE ON BEFORE...

"Hush!" said Grandma. She gripped the wheel tightly.

We drove up and up and up in a tight spiral. My mother clutched the door handle. "Be sure you're wearing your seat belt!" she told me.

(I am still not sure how the seat belt would have helped with a seven-thousand-foot drop off the side of a mountain.)

"Grandma, I'm nearly sure we're on that same road . . ." I said again.

And then suddenly we crested the top of the mountain and there was a spot to pull over. It looked like we were standing on top of the world.

"It *is* beautiful," said my mother. "That man at the gas station was right."

"Of course he was," said Grandma, fluffing her curls. "He liked my hair. Clearly a man of excellent taste."

We opened the door, and the wind howled through the car, grabbing every stray bit of paper, including the map, and flinging it over the edge of the mountain.

I tried to catch the map, but my mom grabbed me because she was afraid I would run off a cliff without my seat belt.

"Well," said Grandma, "there's only one way off the mountain, I guess. We don't need a map for that."

We began the long, long drive down. We were behind a car with a license plate from Nebraska. Nebraska doesn't have mountains, and we wondered what the other driver thought about Beartooth Pass. Since he never went more than fifteen miles per hour, he was probably *extremely* impressed.

* * *

Eventually, with a lot of gas station stops, we reached Wyoming. We were very tired and stayed in a motel for the night.

It was gray and rainy in Wyoming. Mom was still traumatized by Beartooth Pass and wanted to turn around and go home.

It was impossible to keep Grandma down, though. She was determined to go see her oil land. The next morning, she put on a plastic rain bonnet to keep her curls dry, and we set off to find it.

We went on a highway, and then the highway became a gravel road. And then the gravel road became a dirt road. The Crown Victoria rattled and bounced, going

BANG BANG CRACK CRUNCH
BANG CRUNCH THUD

"Are you sure this is the right road?" asked my mother.

"Of course I am!" said Grandma. She was always very certain, particularly when she was wrong. "I got directions at the last gas station."

"Did he want to marry you?" I asked.

"No," said my grandmother. "He was too young for me. But he drew me a map." She held out a sheet of paper with squiggly lines on it.

At last we reached a squiggle on the map. I was expecting to see a sign that said "Grandma's Oil Land." I think she was, too.

But it was just endless flat brown earth.

"Is this it?" asked my mother.

"I guess it is," said Grandma. She tightened her rain bonnet and got out of the car.

It continued to be flat and brown and endless. There weren't even any trees.

My mother and I didn't say anything. Neither of us had any idea what oil land was supposed to look like, but it did not look like this place was going to make anyone rich.

Grandma walked off the road and stood there for a while. Then she came back to the car.

"It's oil land," she said. "It's not supposed to be pretty. You wouldn't want to drill somewhere pretty and ruin it."

She tried to get back into the car, but this was difficult because there were three inches of mud on the undersides of her shoes. She had to scrape them off while rain came into the car.

"It's raining pretty hard," I said.

AND I THINK I JUST SAW LIGHTNING.

Lightning usually strikes the highest thing it can find. Our car was the highest thing for twenty miles in any direction.

"Right!" said Grandma. "I'm sure this is prime oil land. Now let's get out of here."

She started the car, and it went forward a few feet and then went

SQUELL-LL-LL-LL-CH

We stopped moving.

The dirt road had turned to mud. The lightning storm was still coming. And the car was stuck.

"Never say die," said Grandma. She tightened her rain bonnet again and got out of the car. My mother slid behind the wheel.

Grandma opened the trunk and pulled out a cardboard box. It held the glass clown she'd bought in Montana.

She took out the clown and put it

in the backseat

next to me.

It was the kind of clown that shows up in horror movies. I was afraid that if the lightning didn't get us, we'd be eaten by the clown. And I would be unable to get away from it because my mother wouldn't let me unbuckle my seat belt.

Grandma tore the cardboard box in half and put one half under each of the back tires of the car. This was supposed to give it some traction so that it wouldn't sink immediately into the mud.

"Hit it!" she called to my mother.

My mother hit the gas.

The car went

SQUELL-RRNN-RNN-CRUNCH

and jumped forward.

My grandmother vanished with a yelp.

My mother immediately hit the brakes. (She said later that she was convinced she'd killed Grandma.)

Thunder rolled across the landscape. Lightning stabbed the ground.

Covered from head to toe in glop, like a mud-monster rising from the earth, my grandmother stood.

She stomped around the side of the car and opened the door.

"You're alive!" said my mother, sliding back to the passenger side.

"Of course I'm alive," said Grandma. "I just slipped, that's all." She sat down in the driver's seat, getting mud all over the brown velour. "When the car went, I lost my footing and went down in the mud. I'm fine."

She looked down at her muddy self and shook her head.

AT LEAST MY HAIR'S DRY.

My mother and I stared at her. Her rain bonnet was half off, and her amazing permed curls were now coated in a layer of . . . well, of mud from Grandma's oil land.

"Uh," said my mother.

"Um," I said.

Thunder crashed outside.

"It might have gotten a little wet," said my mother tactfully.

Grandma flipped open the little mirror in the visor and looked at it.

There was a long, long silence. Mom and I held our breath. We'd come all this way over scary roads, and the oil land had been disappointing, and Grandma had just kept going. But now her hair was completely ruined.

Grandma started to laugh.

COME ON. LET'S GET OUT OF HERE AND GO GET BRUNCH.

* * *

After we got home, we figured out that the map from the gas station attendant had been wrong. Grandma's oil land had been somewhere else entirely.

"Do . . . do you want to go back?" asked my mother.

Grandma thought about it. She lifted her hand to her hair, which was freshly permed (again) after its Wyoming adventure. The glass clown had been exiled to a display case, and all the mud had been scraped out of the Crown Victoria.

"No," she said decisively. "I've decided I'm opposed to drilling for oil. It's probably bad for the environment or something."

We agreed that this was probably for the best.

One Hot Mess

By Carmen Agra Deedy

When you're a kid you think your family is normal.

You assume *everybody* has a family that celebrates New Year's Day with a Jell-O fight on the lawn, has an aunt who makes aluminum foil jewelry, or sets a fire in the bathtub on moving day.

A little background on that last one.

My parents were Cuban refugees. We grew up in a small Southern town where they worked, paid taxes, and went to church. As far as I could tell, they were pretty ordinary people.

Okay, so maybe my mother liked to clean.

A lot.

She descended from a long line of Iberian women who believed it their mission to rid the world of dirt and grime. In her defense, my mother's grandmother and sister both died of typhoid fever in 1930s Havana. This terrible loss marked the beginning of Mami's life-long campaign against "The Godless Germ." As part of her arsenal, she kept a spray can of Lysol disinfectant tucked in her pocketbook.

"Danger never takes a holiday," my mother would remind my sister and me, as she sprayed down a grocery cart handle, "and nothing is more dangerous than The Godless Germ."

I never thought any of this odd, until the year I turned nine.

It was our fourth move in five years. My dad, Papi, was a steel worker, and money was always tight. We would stay in a place until the rent went up, and then we'd pull up stakes and move into another house— usually no more than two or three blocks and a decade older than the last one.

But this time was different.

Papi's willingness to work extra hours at the steel mill had earned him a raise, and our family the nicest place we had rented yet.

No more crappy old clapboard houses with rusted faucets, warped windowsills, and bathrooms with chipped tiles. No sirree. We were moving into an apartment complex with a flower bed in the parking lot, and a swimming pool.

I remember how excited Mami was when we walked into apartment number eight. It was freshly painted and carpeted, and everything smelled of new-ness with a capital N. Even our battered furniture looked a little brighter. When Papi arrived some ten minutes later with hamburgers from the corner diner, I just knew this day couldn't possibly get any better.

"I'm going back to the house for the last load," announced our father.

"Wait for me!" I shoved the last few bites of greasy burger into my mouth, pushed the chair away from the table, and headed after him. When I stepped outside, a shaggy-haired kid was bouncing an old tennis ball against the wall next to our apartment.

"You moving into number eight?" he asked me.

I beamed at him what I hoped was my most winning "you-bet-I-am-and-is-today-your-lucky-day-or-WHAT-because-you-get-dibs-on-the-new-kid" smile. I followed it up with, "You wanna watch my mom set fire to the bathtub?"

He just stared at me with luminescent green eyes that reminded me of winter antifreeze. Then, in infinitesimal increments—like molasses seeping from a broken jar along a cold winter floor, one millimeter at a time—a smile spread across his face. It kept spreading, until it bunched up his cheeks and reached his eyes. Then, and only then, did he speak.

"Boy howdy, do I!"

"Great," I cried. "Come on! She's almost ready."

He followed me into the apartment without hesitation. I watched him take in the neat rows of labeled boxes, the cheap Naugahyde recliner, the shiny Formica kitchen table. A perplexed look settled on his face.

"So, is your mama a pyro? 'Cause this don't look like no pyro's house; you still got plenty of stuff that'll burn."

"What's a *pie-row*?" I asked.

"Somebody who lights stuff on fire so's they can watch it burn."

"No! My mom doesn't like to watch the bathtub *burn*. She likes to watch the germs *die*."

"She—say *what*?"

The look on his face made that hastily eaten burger stir treacherously in my stomach.

Until that instant, I'd genuinely believed that everyone's mother did this. A hot, prickly sensation crept its way up my neck. I recognized it for what it was: shame. *Burning a bathtub was weird.*

"L-l-let me explain," I stammered.

"I cain't wait to hear."

So I told him.

I told him about my mother's dead grandmother and sister back in Cuba. I told him about the spray can of Lysol in her pocketbook. I told him the world was filled with all manner of invisible bugs just waiting to eat out your brains and turn your guts to mush and kill you deader than dead with just an innocent swipe of a doorknob.

And when I finished telling, do you know what he did?

He laughed.

He laughed so hard he wheezed.

He laughed so long he swallowed his gum and coughed it back up again.

And do you know what I did?

I punched him in the arm.

He stumbled sideways, dropped dramatically to the floor, and laughed harder.

"Easy, girl. You got a mean right hook there." The words were spoken between fits and starts of more hilarity.

"What is going on here . . . ?" Mami stood in the doorway and looked from me to this alien child and back again.

"He's my friend," I said. "His name is . . ." I lowered my voice. "What's your name?"

"My name's Ronald, ma'am. Wayne Ronald Harding, but ever'body calls me Ronald." My mother nodded, as if this was enough information for anybody. Then she turned to me and said, "I find the matches. The bathtub, she burn in ten minutes." She said this in accented English, and I was relieved when she turned on her heel and disappeared down the short hall.

"This is kinda crazy, huh?" I said.

"It's better'n crazy. This here's an *opportunity*."

Ronald leaned toward me and whispered, "Let's sell tickets."

And that's what we did.

Ronald rustled up a half dozen of his friends and told them that, for a quarter, they'd see something worth telling their grandchildren about someday. I stood in front of the door to number eight and explained what was about to happen to the small but eager crowd.

First, I said, my mom would scrub the bathtub with a bristle brush. Then she'd make certain there was nothing flammable in the room. As an added precaution, she'd place a bucket of water on the toilet. Next, she'd screw off the lid of a sixteen-ounce bottle of isopropyl alcohol and cover the tub's surface.

Then, and only then, would she strike the match and toss it in. I'd seen her do it time and again. It was a marvelous sight. Those old ceramic tubs would burst into flames, and just as quickly the fire would burn itself out.

"Now, I ask you," said Ronald, to the dumbstruck congregation, "ain't that the dangdest thing y'all ever heard? So, who's in?" Kids tripped over one another to hand over their quarters.

Mami was visibly startled when she saw me coming down the hall, a mob of children following along behind.

"Can they watch, too?" I gave her a pleading look.

She looked at the kids and shook her head. "Ay, ay, ay." But then she put aside whatever misgivings she may have had; she had work to do. The Godless Germ waits for no woman, and we had to have baths that night. She addressed the crowd.

"Okay, childrens. You no go in bathroom. You stay in door. NO GO IN. ¿Me comprenden?"

Whether they understood or not, no one was leaving. No one was *breathing*. This was a tale, as Ronald had promised, that they would tell their grandchildren. Unbeknownst to them, this was their Saint Crispin's Day.

My mother unscrewed the top of the bottle of alcohol.

She moved the bucket of water closer to the tub.

She upturned the bottle and drained the contents with great care.

She reached into her apron pocket and drew from it a small box of wooden matches.

The crowd pressed forward.

"¡Tranquilos!"

Again, no one moved. But all eyes watched as she struck the match and tossed it in a perfect flaming arc into the bathtub.

The brand-spanking-new FIBERGLASS bathtub.

The thing lit up like kerosene-soaked kindling.

The plastic melted and warped as the fire spread.

Kids began to shriek as they scattered in a panic for the front door. Only three people held their ground: my mother, who flipped on the bathroom faucet and splashed bucket after bucket onto the flames; me, too terrified to run, or scream, or be of any use to anyone whatsoever; and Ronald. Well . . . Ronald actually disappeared briefly. He returned moments later, followed by a man in a ribbed white T-shirt who was carrying a fire extinguisher.

Within seconds the bathroom was a blanket of white foam, giving the room the look of a peaceful, if bizarre, Christmas postcard—so long as you were unaware of the horror that lay beneath.

"Now, that is one hot mess, ma'am," said the man with the fire extinguisher. "I just gotta ask. What in the world made you want to light a tub on fire?" The soft, unflustered voice and the strange color of his eyes hinted at what Ronald would look like in about twenty years.

"She had to kill The Godless Germ," I said.

He nodded. "Well, I reckon that explains it about as well as anything."

*   *   *

None of the apartment kids were allowed to play with me after that day. Heck, they weren't even allowed to pass my door without an escort.

Except for Ronald.

When he showed up the next morning, I was sitting in the doorway, picking at a scab.

"Hey!"

"I'm surprised your parents let you talk to me," I said.

"Ain't got parents; got a dad. You met him. He's a firefighter, down Ladder 11 way. He said to call him if anything else catches fire. He and the boys'll be down here in a tick."

"You're not funny." My face felt as hot as melting fiberglass.

Ronald squatted in front of me, where I couldn't avoid looking at him, and said, "You know, I had me an uncle once who swore up and down that for every lie I told, Santa Claus would have to eat one of his reindeer."

"That's crazy—" I stopped cold and looked into those extraordinary eyes.

"It's only crazy," he said, *"when somebody else's family does it."*

And I knew then that Wayne Ronald Harding and I would be friends forever.

Or at least until the rent went up again.

Fleamail

By Deborah Underwood

Dear Rover,

I read your advice column all the time. Telling that cat who wanted attention to unroll all the toilet paper in the bathroom was brilliant! I've spread the word to all my kitty friends.

But now I need your help. I am a cat in a shelter. How do I get someone to adopt me?
Love,
Bella

Dear Bella,

Good question! First, you need to look adorable. Make sure you're well-groomed. Do you have a cute meow? Use it! And if the person comes in to visit you, purr and curl up in her lap. You can play a little, but most people like quiet, calm pets. Good luck!
Love,
Rover

Dear Rover,

Thank you! Someone wonderful came in today! She had a purple shirt that said "Pet Power," so I think we'll get along just fine. She's checking with her mom right now. Any other tips?

Love,

Bella

Dear Bella,

I'm so glad you found someone you—

Wait. A purple "Pet Power" shirt? Was she wearing sparkly silver sneakers?

Love,

Rover

Dear Rover,

Yes! They smelled like dog, but that's okay—I like dogs! Anyway, what else should I do?

Love,

Bella

Dear Bella,

Claw at her jeans. And run around the cage meowing at the top of your lungs. And then hock a nice, big hairball.

Love,

Rover

Dear Rover,
Really??
Love,
Bella

Dear Bella,
Yes.
Love,
Rover

Dear Rover,
Okay. I did it. Now she and her mom are talking with the
shelter staff. They look worried. Anything else?
Love,
Bella

Dear Bella,
Barf. Right on the silver sneakers.
Love,
Rover

Dear Rover,
Are you sure? I thought they hated that.
Love,
Bella

Bella:
Trust me.
Rover

* * *

Bella,
What's going on?

* * *

Bella,
I need an update!

Dearest Rover,
You are so smart! It totally worked! Her mom is really
worried about me now, and says the shelter must be
stressing me out. They were going to wait till the
weekend to bring me home, but now they're going to pick
me up tonight!
I would have never done the vomiting and hairball
and screeching without you. I would have just rubbed
against her legs and purred and been cute, and that
wouldn't have worked at all. You are the best!
Love,
Bella

Three Days Later . . .

Dear Rover,

It is silly that I have to fleamail you when we're living in the same house. How was I supposed to know she was YOUR person?

You've been under that bed for three days. You can't stay there forever.

Love,

Bella

Dear Bella,

Yes, I can.

Rover

Dear Rover,

You'll have to come out to pee.

Bella

Dear Bella,

Nope.

R

Dear Rover,

Oh. That's what all the yelling was about.

Look. What's the problem? Come out and say hi. It's

not like you're afraid of cats, right? (Haha!)
Bella

B,
No comment.
R

Dear Rover,
Seriously?? You weigh TEN TIMES more than I do!
What do you think I'm going to do—bite you with my
poisonous fangs?
Bella

B,
YOU HAVE POISONOUS FANGS???????
I KNEW IT!!!
R

Dear Rover,
Oh, good grief. Of course I don't. I'm not a snake! Even I
am scared of those.

Look, maybe I can help you. Did you ever think about
that? What if a cat needs advice about which things to
knock off the kitchen counter? What if a dog needs tips
on getting along with his new feline housemate (ahem)?
Having dog and cat viewpoints would make your
column even better.

Meet me by the food bowls. Please? I'll let you have one of my treats.
Bella

B—
No, I—wait. Did you say treats? The liver-flavored ones?
R

Dear Rover,
Yes. BUT JUST ONE.
Bella

One hour later . . .

Dear Bella,
Thank you for the treats. I'm sorry I ate all of them. What can I say? I'm a dog.
I'm glad we're friends now. Do you want to come outside and sniff other dogs' butts with me?
Love,
Rover

Dear Rover,
I'm glad we're friends, too. But, no. No, I do not.
Love,
Bella

The next week . . .

Dear Bella and Rover,

I am a python in a shelter. There's a nice kid who wants to adopt me. How do I make a good impression?

Love,

Penny

Dear Penny,

Rover here. First, you need to look adorable. Make sure you're well-groomed. Do you—HEY!

(Sorry, Rover.) Penny, this is Bella. What is the girl wearing? This is VERY, VERY IMPORTANT. Tell us, then we'll tell you what to do next.

Bella and **Rover**

Dear Bella and Rover,

It's not a girl. It's a boy. And he's wearing a green T-shirt. Why?

Love,

Penny

Dear Penny,

Whew. I mean . . . no reason. We were just curious. Right, Rover?

Right. Penny, just be your lovely, snakelike self. Any other advice, Bella?

Barf on his shoes. It worked for me!

Love,
Bella and **Rover**

A MOST SERIOUS RECITATION OF THE POEM "Trees" BY JOYCE KILMER

• • • • • • • • •

RENDERED MOST SERIOUSLY (and with utmost care) BY THE HAND OF Cece Bell!

HI. I'M JOYCE KILMER.

YES, *I KNOW* THAT "JOYCE" IS A GIRL'S NAME.

WANNA MAKE SOMETHING OF IT?

I FEEL AS IF MY POEM HAS BEEN DISPARAGED IN THESE PAGES.

I WOULD LIKE TO SHARE IT WITH YOU NOW, IN ITS ENTIRETY.

"TREES," BY ME.

I think that I shall never see

A poem lovely as a—

HEY, LOOK! IT'S BOB FRANKLIN, READING THAT CRAZY *PEE POEM* AGAIN! YOU'LL *LOVE* IT!

the END!

Things Could Be Verse

By Kelly DiPucchio

Bad Hair Day

Mary found a little hair.
It's long and black as night.
When Mary saw it way down *THERE*
it gave her quite a fright.

Mary had one single thought:
How did it grow so fast?!
There was no hair the day before.
The girl was flabbergast!

Everywhere that Mary went
that hair was sure to go.
Thank goodness for her socks and shoes.
The hair was on her toe.

My Secret

Today I'm shopping for a bra.
I can hardly wait!
I've been dreaming of this fancy store
since the age of eight.

One bra has that push-up stuff.
Another, moving parts.
A third bra comes with batteries
to light the flashing hearts.
This one has long tasseled ends.
That one has a pouch.
This one's in a floral print
that looks like Grandma's couch.
This bra's WAY too pointy.
And where's the shoulder strap?
The next one's complicated—
They should call it BOOBY TRAP.
I kind of like the cheetah bra,
but Mom is mouthing "NO!"
Instead, she picks the pastel pink
with the baby bow.
I really love the feathered one.
"It's see-through!" Mother said.

Check out *these* cup sizes!
They could cover my whole head!
There's loads of lace throughout this place.
It's itchy, I can tell.
I'm starting to feel woozy
from the store's perfume-y smell.

My dream's become a nightmare.
These sizes are so dumb!
I think I've had enough for now—
Sports bras, here I come!

Breakaway

The game begins. I start to sweat.
The opposing team looms large.
I plot my course and gather force
and then begin my charge.

Weaving 'cross the playing field
my focus is intense.
My only chance of winning
is a bold and brave offense.

Soon, I'm checked and then I'm decked.
A forward kicks my shin.

Here comes a six-foot stopper
with an evil, twisted grin.

Dodge left.
Dart right.
I see an open hole!
My heart starts beating faster.
I'm almost at the goal!

I'm tripped!
Shirt rips!
Someone call a foul!
I scramble to get up again
as fullbacks near me scowl.

At last I'm there, with sweat-drenched hair
outsmarting one last blocker.
Every day's a ruthless match
when racing to my locker.

Swimming Is
for Other Kids

By Akilah Hughes

My only good experiences with water have taken place on the beach or in the shower. Swimming pools—in any form—are the bane of my existence.

I was by far the smallest kid in third grade—under four feet tall—and I had the swimming ability of an Olympic rock. Liquid just wasn't my thing. It wasn't that I didn't want to learn. I had even gone to swim class. I simply couldn't master the kicking or the arm stroking, and when I tried to float, I sank to the bottom every time.

"Must be genetic," my mother said. She spent most of her pool time reading magazines and catnapping in the sun. I think I saw her walk into the water a total of once.

One summer day at the Boys & Girls Club, I was put to the test.

There's this game called Chicken Fight, which requires neither legitimate fight training nor chickens. You just climb on your friend's shoulders and another duo does the same, and the girls on the shoulders grab each other's hands and try to rip them off of their wrists. The first one to fall into the water loses.

Kasey had asked me to sit on her shoulders, and no way was I going to chicken out. (See what I did there?) Also, it would be interesting to see the world from the perspective of an adult, rather than basically a toddler.

She waited in the water below for me to back my little butt over her head and onto her shoulders. Kasey was tall and broad, having hit puberty earlier than the rest of us. She got all the perks. Her body was basically that of a twenty-three-year-old. She was the only girl who could wear a two-piece without looking like she was playing dress-up in her mom's suit. And, no, I wasn't jealous. Kasey wanted *me* as her chicken partner, and *I* wanted people to associate her womanly finesse and bosom with my . . . less impressive body.

"Are you getting in or not? We're losing time, Hughes!" she yelled.

Backing into a pool—backing into a pool and *getting on top of someone's shoulders*—when you're no better a swimmer than an anchor was daunting at best, and next-level horrifying at worst. I kept thinking about falling in, and then what I would do if we didn't win the chicken fight. Would I be the biggest loser at the Club? Would Kasey let me drown because I'd embarrassed her? Would I live to fill an A-cup?

I got on, grabbing Kasey's hair for leverage.

"Stop pulling my hair! Ow! What is happening?!" were the last words I heard before I hit the water.

Then a whistle blew. Our pool time was up.

Frantically, I tried to ascend to the surface and make it back to the wall, but sinking to death seemed to be my only true skill set. I jumped up and down in the water and screamed, "Help!" before swallowing another mouthful of chlorine. I had to do it at least four times before the lifeguard finally noticed, dove in, and towed me back to the side of the pool.

I couldn't stop crying. Partially from the near-death experience in the 4.5-foot section of the pool. Partially from shame; how could I lose at Chicken Fight before round one started? Why didn't Kasey try to save me or, at the very least, wait to find out that I hadn't drowned in the community pool? Oh, and why was I so absurdly short that no one would ever ask me to play any pool games with them ever again?

After that I stopped venturing into pools. But it turned out that even being *near* a pool was dangerous enough.

* * *

By the time I hit fourteen, I had blossomed. Though I didn't look like Kasey, I was a nearly normal-sized human. I wasn't confident in my body yet (even though my little tummy from a diet of mostly chips was pretty adorable in hindsight), but when my friend Ali invited me over to "float on floaties" in her backyard pool, I wore a two-piece anyway, excited for my stomach to match the color of my arms for the first summer in my life.

When I arrived on Saturday in my dazzling purple bikini, carrying an abundance of Doritos, at least half my classmates were there. This, I had not expected.

Ali was cool, sure, but she wasn't *popular*. The fact that her crush (plus every potential object of freshman year infatuation) was there, splashing around, confirmed my long-held suspicion that one's high school popularity was directly related to their house's capacity for parties. Ali's basically made her a shoo-in for prom queen, student body president, and eventually commander in chief of the United States.

I dropped my chip bounty at the snack table and unrolled my towel on a beach chair near the water.

"Hey, girl!" Ali yelled from a flamingo floatie. "Jump right in. The water's *fine!*" But it *wasn't* fine. I approached the side of the pool, flashing back to tiny, doofus Akilah playing chicken against an empty swimming pool and basically losing and dying back in elementary school.

"I'm all good, Al!" I said, trying to sound chipper about the party, given that I'd thought today was going to be only the two of us hanging out.

Just then, Ali's older, unfairly beautiful brother Brad screamed, "CAN-NON-BALLLLL!" and at full speed and circumference turned into a human weapon, causing what is still the largest wave of my life. I was certain that everyone within a three-mile radius had been in the splash zone, and that the pool was completely emptied by his attack.

Wiping my eyes to assess the damage, I heard, "WHOA!" followed by maniacal boy laughter. I started laughing, too . . . and then a sudden breeze hit me like a beach ball.

My gorgeous purple bikini, which was only supposed to be seen by Ali and a handful of Cool Ranch chips, had become a monokini. That is to say, I was topless. In front of most, if not all, of the freshman class.

I grabbed my towel and sprinted indoors, forgetting that my clothes were outside and my bikini top was still missing in action. I ran to Ali's room, throwing on whatever T-shirt and cheer shorts I could find, and then started the short, barefoot walk home. By the time I got there, my mother had returned from work, confused about why I wasn't at Ali's anymore.

"Wardrobe malfunction, Mom," I told her, and given her neutrality about water, we changed topics.

The rest of my summer was spent living down the incident, reading books on dry land, and watching Nickelodeon from the couch. I realized that *that's* who I was. My best life will be lived warm and dry, away from parties, fun, and freshman boys.

So, basically, pools are a death sentence. If you need me, I'll be lying facedown on a beach towel, trying to forget everything you just read.

Dear Bella and Rover

By Deborah Underwood

Dear Bella and Rover,
I am a parrot. My name is Polly. My people keep asking if I
want a cracker. My cage is full of crackers. I hate
crackers! Please help. These guys are driving me . . .
well, crackers.
Love,
Polly

Dear Polly,
Really? You don't like crackers? I love crackers! I
especially like the ones with sesame seeds on them.
And the ones—

Sorry about that, Polly. Rover doesn't understand,
because dogs will eat anything. A certain dog I know—
AHEM—ate a shoe last night. But I get it. I won't even
eat my favorite food half the time, because I like to keep
the two-leggers guessing.

I suggest you try negative reinforcement. Every time they ask if you want a cracker, make the sound of a dentist's drill. "Polly want a cracker?"

"BZZZZZZZZZZ!"

"Polly want a cracker?"

"BZZZZZZZZZZ!"

I bet they'll stop asking really fast. Any more advice, Rover?

Yes! If you get more crackers, can you send them to me? Please?

Love,

Bella and **Rover**

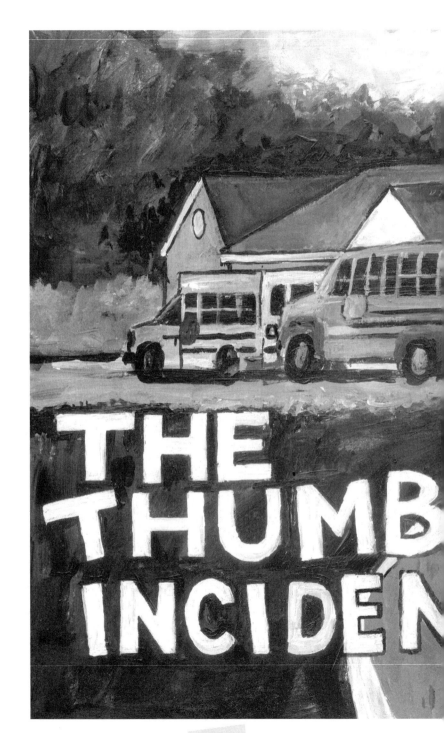

THE
THUMB
INCIDEN

A TRUE STORY BY
MEGHAN MCCARTHY

When I was in elementary school, I got the chance to staple stuff to the bulletin board.

I was already a master with the stapler.

I got lots of practice, as the class often had staple fights.

PING!

OW!

The bulletin board was a chance for me to have more fun with the stapler. Perhaps I'd become a little TOO confident...

POP

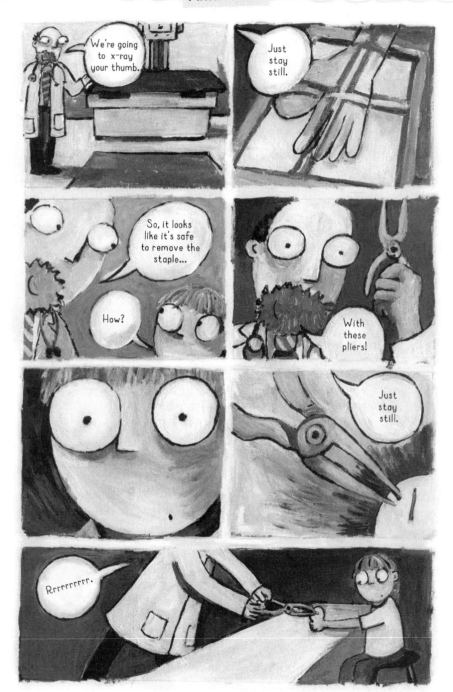

Desdemona and Sparks Go All In

By Rita Williams-Garcia and Michelle Garcia

"I-got-it-I-got-it-I-got-it!"

I've been on the "What now?" end of this friendship since second grade. Forty-three mad schemes later, I still ask, "What now?"

"Dez, I've got the answer to our problem. The solution to our X, that's what!" Sparks is doing the awkgly dance that makes her my eternal bestie. It's. So. Embarrassing. And in the lunchroom, no less. The more I look on in horror, the more she cranks it up. Sparks just doesn't care.

We've been plotting our way into Prep, the passport to our dream schools, for the past sixteen months. Our task? To make our applications stand out in a school of standouts, where every person is vying to be among the 35 percent. Our middle school is the unofficial sister school to Prep, but that doesn't guarantee an "in." It doesn't take much to crack the admissions matrix: Out of an incoming class of ninety, they take 35 percent from our school, 30 percent from the parochials and charters, 15 percent homeschoolers, 10 percent public schoolers, and 10 percent celeb brats. All we need is one ridiculously outstanding thing to both put us in and make us rise above the likely 35 percent. The solve-for-X factor's hard to come up with when our entire graduating class has pretty much the same application: 3.89 GPA or better, athletes, mathletes, first chair violin—or musical equivalent—and being really close to ending world hunger with an ethical but great tasting globally satisfying grain. Extra points if you have your own .org.

Sparks stops awk-gly dancing in mid flap. "Behold," she says, framing her head. "In here lies the answer to our problems."

"Okay . . ."

"Ellen," she says. Then hops. "Ellen!"

"Ellen?"

"Ellen." She nods like I know this Ellen. And then the lightbulb clicks on.

"You mean *Ellen*, of *The Ellen DeGeneres Show*?"

"What other Ellen matters? Don't you see? It's perfect. Ellen will get us into Prep."

I shake my head no, no, and no—tight, no-nonsense no's so there's no miscommunication. She shakes hers yes, many yeses with all-out loosey-goosey up-and-down swan neck action. Suddenly, the thing I love most about Sparks flies out the window. I grab her shoulders with both hands. "Stop it. Lunchroom!" But it's Sparks Freeman, and she doesn't care.

"We go on *Ellen*, list our appearance on our 'Special Talents and Citations' section, and we're in. Think, Dez! Who else will have that on their application?"

"How is that even a plan? We somehow get on *The Ellen DeGeneres Show*, hope Prep's selection committee watches and worships Ellen, and then hope they remember us for doing, like, who knows what, and *then* we're in Prep? Really?"

"And yet, that's how it'll all go down! Let's move on this and make it happen." Her face is deadpan serious.

I pick up my phone and fake hit up some numbers. "'Hello, guest booking person for *Ellen*? You know how Beyoncé and the pope are booked for next week? Can we bump them for Desdemona and Sparkle from the Middle School for the Gifted? . . . That's right. Just five minutes . . . Tuesday? I'll see if they're available.'"

"What you sound like is a crazy person. What I'm saying makes complete sense."

"Sure it does, and for our special talent we'll break down some geometry problems on daytime TV."

"Or," Sparks says calmly, to make me sound like the crazy one, "we'll perform our champion birdcalling talent."

"Our bird—WHAT?" I leave out *champion*. It's as nonexistent as our birdcalling talent.

She gives me a disappointed look and blows a puff of canned cling peaches breath in my face. "For such a nerd, you're being really dense right now. Look, the national birdcalling competition's coming up. We enter. We win. We're invited to go on *Ellen*. We add it to our application, and we're in." She says this like she's saying, "Let's get burritos."

It doesn't matter. Mad scheme number forty-four will have to be mad without me. "No."

Now she starts flapping and hopping. In the lunchroom. People still eating. Now definitely gawking. "Caw-caw-cawmon. C'mon, c'mon. Caw!"

It works. "Will you stop?"

"If you say you're down," she says. "And the best part is, Ellen's always booking viral acts. She asks fans to submit their talents."

True confession: on Fridays Sparks and I skip lunch to watch *Ellen* in the media center.

I roll my eyes. A weak yes. "I guess if we're going to do this, we'd better start researching," I say.

"Research? We've got this! Find some cool birds on YouTube. I'll take the high pitch. You take the low."

I just stare. She stares right back, like, *why aren't we watching bird clips already?*

This is a waste of time. We should be finding a cure for pinkeye or something impressive. I've scoped out the competition. Gina Two Nose Jobs (separate lacrosse incidents) got written up in the free local papers for her fruit fly genome thing. She's in. Eduardo spent his summer building mold-free homes in Guatemala. He's in. Irma Krishnaswami's mother is on the board at Prep. In. And *our* grand plan to get in? Birdcalling. On *Ellen*.

Little-known fact: Sparks's mom named her Sparkle after both the paper towels and this movie about an R & B girl group. Her mom laughs at Sparks's fund to legally change her name to Ann, the most Sparkle-free name she could think of. Not even an *e* on the end. What Mrs. Freeman doesn't know is, Sparks plans to sue her for personal injury and for ruining her future career possibilities with a name like Sparkle. She's citing her favorite read, *Freakonomics*.

I'm not worried about being Desdemona Brown. At least the admissions committee will know my mom read *Othello*.

"Now that you're in, really in," Sparks says, "we have to draft a third member. The standout birdcalling groups come in threes."

"You mean get someone else to risk their application, go on national daytime television, and—"

"Lock in their spot at Prep?"

I feel her forehead for a fever. She sidesteps my hand. "Stop it, Dez. People will think we're weird."

"Too late."

"Will you be serious?" How do I respond to that? But she means it. "Who can we get as our third? Someone who's down, but won't steal the spotlight from us. She's got to be good. Good enough to help us win, but without deflecting attention from us."

"You mean a utility birdcaller?"

"Exactly."

We take a minute. While I fantasize about pulling out of mad scheme forty-four, Sparks racks her brain for a possible third. Her eyes light up and then narrow conspiratorially.

"Irma Krishnaswami."

I shake my head. "And risk ... risk ..." I stop myself. Lightbulb! She's right. Irma's already in. She'd risk nada. And Irma's always easing her way into our circle of two.

*   *   *

We commit to the plan and enlist Krishnaswami. We actually prepare to be talented birdcallers. Together, we huddle, plot, and mimic birdcalls we find on YouTube. We look for a bird to mimic in our hood, but dirty pigeons, sparrows, and the occasional crow are too cool to sing for us. When they do sing, it's not impressive. I suggest we come up with a different talent. But then—

"I-got-it-I-got-it-I-got-it!"

Oh, good. "What?"

"We use the sounds of the neighborhood to create our own bird. And then we give it a super ridiculous bird name, like the . . . urban gray-breasted . . ."

I add, "Plover . . ."

Krishnaswami adds, "Jay of prey!"

"But shouldn't it be a real bird?" I ask.

"Look, Dez. This is our shot."

Krishnaswami backs Sparks like crazy. "It's creative, and Ellen will get a kick out of it. Besides. Who's going to check? The birdcalling police?" She and Sparks fist-bump, ending in two hands flying away.

* * *

So here is what happens.

We do an analysis of the types of talented fans that Ellen has picked to appear on her show. From there, we create a prediction matrix to better guess which talents she's likely to book on her show as each week goes by.

Sparks opens an Instagram account for our urban gray-breasted plover jay of prey. We get hits. We Photoshop our jay of prey's natural urban habitat. (The UGB-

PJP prefers the Key Food and Trader Joe's roofs for nesting. More chances to dive for free samples.) Most importantly we study the art of making ugly faces, as well as the timing of unpredictable bird sounds. In no time, our UGBPJP sounds like the Mister Softee ice cream truck song, a volunteer ambulance truck, and the phlegm-clearing old guy across the street who is also my 6:45 alarm. We practice like maniacs. All together, we create bird pandemonium.

After two months of dedicated practice we compete for the national birdcalling championship. Our entry is swiftly disqualified.

That's okay. We move on to phase two of our grand plan to get into Prep. We shoot this incredible submission tape and send it to Ellen. According to our talent prediction matrix, we should get a call from Ellen's producers within the next three weeks. Tops.

The producers from *Ellen* do not call.

Still, it turns out our matrix was pretty good. We know this because we snuck out to the media center and turned on *The Ellen DeGeneres Show*, and who are Ellen's special talented fan guests? A group of local amateur birdcallers. How local? One block south of the street where we live. No doubt we inspired them. They're boring though. They just make pigeon noises.

We are outraged. Sparks phones the producers and

demands equal time. They say it's too soon to put on another birdcalling group. They're nice about it. "Keep trying. Maybe next year."

Too late for us.

"Oh, well," Krishnaswami says. "At least it was fun."

Krishnaswami gets her letter. Well, her text from her mom. She's in.

The birdcallers who stole our idea and made it on *Ellen*? They're now the voices behind a start-up video game. About birds.

Sparks is inconsolable. I catch her dipping into her personal injury lawsuit fund for emergency nacho binges. She suggests we sign up for judo so we can survive the halls of any school that isn't Prep. She types "Sparkle Freeman" on her homework. And exams.

Time passes, and we heal. A little. We send our applications to our backup schools and we say mean things about Ellen, even though we still sneak to the media center to catch a few minutes of the show. We gain perspective. Sparks admits it was a long shot.

Then Krishnaswami says, "Have you seen this?"

"Seen what?"

"We've gone viral!"

She holds up the phone. Someone from *Ellen* posted our audition tape on YouTube. It's received 350,000 views in one week—more than the actual birdcalling group that got to be on the show. A DJ in Los Angeles mashed up our birdcalling pandemonium with a Katy Perry song. And the YouTube comments aren't even all that mean! Some people like my ice cream truck wailing. Some can't get over Krishnaswami's throat clearing. *How can all of that come out of such a small girl?*

But the big hit? Sparks's half ambulance, half caw-caw, complete with her crazy awk-gly bird dance. At this point, I'm over Prep and viral fame. On the upside, we still have options for our fallback schools, so I'm not worried. Sooner or later, Sparkle Freeman and I will be on the same page.

7 Things I THOUGHT WERE (THINK are) FUNNY

... BUT WERE REALLY KIND of SAD, and THAT ALL HAPPENED TO MY LITTLE BROTHER, by Lisa BROWN *

* WITH THANKS and APOLOGIES TO MY BELOVED BROTHER

Babysitting Nightmare

By Shannon Hale

Mrs. Grady got my number from a friend of a friend of a friend of my mother's. I should've realized that meant she'd already gone through all the babysitters in her own neighborhood. But I needed the money. I was saving up for science camp.

Besides, I'd been babysitting for two years already. There was nothing I couldn't handle. So I put on my white linen shirt to look professional and packed my babysitter bag with picture books, crafts, and my trusty cow puppet.

"That one's Greta and that one's Henna," said Mrs. Grady when we got to her house. The twins were playing with Legos on the carpet in absolute silence. Four-year-old girls, curly black hair, Greta dressed in green and Henna in red. They were adorable, like little Christmas elves. This job was going to be a piece of cake.

"Dinner's on the stove. They can have a cookie for dessert. Bedtime's at seven thirty; I'll be back at ten. So . . . good luck!" said Mrs. Grady. And then she ran. Literally ran out the front door to where Mr. Grady was waiting in the car, engine running. Usually moms give hugs and kisses and wave from the car and stuff like that. It occurred to me that the Gradys probably didn't go out much. And maybe that was because they couldn't find babysitters. And maybe that was because . . .

I looked at Greta and Henna. They were looking at me. They blinked at the same time.

"I'm Lucía," I said.

"We know," said Greta in green.

"We've been waiting," said Henna in red.

For some reason, I got goose bumps all over my arms.

Henna brought me a book and pushed me toward the couch. "Read!" she said.

No problem! This was going well! Until I realized Greta had disappeared.

"Greta?" I called out.

She called from the bathroom. "I went poop! Come and wipe meeeee!"

But as soon as I got into the bathroom, she ran away with no pants on, yelling, "You can't catch me. I'm the Ginger Batman!"

I chased, really hoping she wouldn't sit down anywhere.

Meanwhile, Henna was screaming my name. "Lucía! Lucía! Lucía!"

As soon as I'd caught Greta, wiped her, and washed my hands, I ran back to the kitchen.

"What? What's wrong?" I asked.

Henna was just standing there, staring at the refrigerator, her bottom lip trembling. "Lucía?" Henna said in a hoarse whisper. "The fridge is looking at me."

Greta took Henna's hand. "It sees us. The fridge sees us."

Goose bumps again. I turned slowly and peeked at the fridge. A totally normal fridge, not looking at anybody. I sighed and turned back. They were gone. In that moment, I learned an important lesson: never, ever turn your back on four-year-old twins.

Eventually I found them in their parents' room. Greta had already wrapped half a roll of Scotch tape around her legs.

"Did you know mummies are real?" she asked. "But their eyeballs dried up and fell out."

Henna was hiding under the bed, whispering, "I'm hungry. I'm hungry and I see your toes."

Goose bumps.

I tried to entertain them with some Candy Land,

the books I'd brought, a tissue paper craft, but an hour later I was running out of ideas. And also free space in my bladder. I'd drunk, like, a quart of chocolate milk at home.

"I need to go potty," I said.

Henna stuck out her tongue and went *pbbbt*. "That's how our tongue goes potty."

"You can go." Greta smiled, showing all her teeth. "We won't do anything naughty."

I didn't dare to go potty.

Instead I spent the next half hour as a human shield, putting myself between the twins while they tried to hit each other with boxes of cereal.

"I'm going to pull off your skin!" Greta screamed at Henna.

"I'm going to bite off your fingers!" Henna screamed at Greta.

"Aah!" I said. "You are so creepy! Why can't you just call each other poopyheads like other kids?"

There was a rare, brief silence. And then . . .

"POO-PEE HEAD!" they shouted at each other. And then at me. At the table. At the cat, who was shivering behind the couch.

They were so busy yelling poopyhead at everything in the house I thought I could sneak to the bathroom. But while I was in there, they stopped yelling poopyhead. I got a cold, sinking feeling in my gut.

I've never peed so fast in my life. I rushed back into the family room. The girls startled.

"We're not doing anything!" said Henna.

"We're not!" said Greta.

That sinking feeling sunk even deeper.

I peeked into the toy box. It was full of water. The toys were floating.

"What did you do?" I wailed.

"We made an aca-quarium!" said Henna proudly.

Greta lifted up a sopping wet teddy bear. "But bears can't swim," she said. "Poor little bear."

Henna whispered, "He drowned."

While I bailed out the toy box, the girls went ahead and ate their allotted cookies. Plus a bonus cookie.

"More cookies," said Henna.

"You already had two cookies. No more now, okay?"

Henna glared at me from beneath lowered eyebrows. "You should say yes." She walked away and looked back over her shoulder. "Remember what happened to Mr. Bear?"

I let her have another cookie.

Eventually, dinner happened. Probably best not to get into details. I may have cried a little. Spaghetti sauce doesn't stain white linen shirts, does it?

Science camp, I reminded myself. *Just remember, it's all for science camp.*

While I was scraping spaghetti out of the curtains, the girls sneaked out the front door.

I caught them two blocks away, still running. Good thing I've been exercising because I had to carry them both back. And they're squirmy.

"Stop cruckeling me!" yelled Henna.

"I don't know what cruckeling means," I said.

"Cruckeling is like scrumping but harder!" yelled Greta.

I locked the front door and barricaded it with kitchen chairs, grabbed their pajamas, and tried to get them dressed. The Tickle Monster trick worked with Henna—who said she loves monsters—but not Greta.

"Come here, Greta," I said. I didn't have the strength to chase her again. My legs felt like cooked noodles.

Greta danced away from me and into the kitchen, waving her arms into the air and humming.

"Greta, bring your rear end over here right now," I said, trying to sound like my mom.

"What's a rear end?" Greta asked.

"It's your . . . you know, your butt."

"This?" asked Greta, wiggling it at me.

"That's not her butt," said Henna. "That's her bum."

"They're the same thing," I said.

"No, they're not!" said Greta.

"Yeah, a butt is yucky and a bum is gross!" said Henna.

Greta began to sob. "You don't like me! You don't like my bum! YOU DON'T LIKE MY BUUUMMM!!"

"Good grief!" I said. My mom said that a lot, and I was beginning to understand why.

I promised them we could watch one short show before bed if Greta would let me get her into pajamas.

I turned on the show and collapsed onto the couch, thinking I might have a chance to catch my breath. Every few seconds one girl would run back into the kitchen and stuff another cookie into her mouth. I pretended not to notice.

When the show was over, I pulled out my secret weapon: the cow puppet. No one can resist the cow puppet.

"You twooo look like goooood girls," I made the puppet say. "Time for bed, mooo!"

They stared, unblinking.

"I eat cows," said Henna.

"On hamburger buns," said Greta.

I swear I felt the puppet tremble.

For its own safety, I stuffed the puppet back into my bag and I herded the girls into their room myself.

"Can I have another cookie?" asked Henna.

"There aren't any more cookies," I said. "You guys ate them all."

"No more cookies?" Her face turned red. She

screamed, "NOW THE WORLD WILL BURN!"

"What? What are you talking about?"

"Uh-oh, Henna is sad. Better give her five more minutes to play," said Greta. "Or, you know, the world will burn."

Okay, five more minutes. Which turned into a hit-Lucía-over-the-head-with-pillows game.

"That's it," I said, rubbing my head. "Now it's really, really time for bed."

"Five more minutes," said Henna.

"We already did five more minutes," I said.

"Sixteen more minutes," said Henna.

Greta flopped around on the floor, rolling back and forth. "I don't have any bones. So oozy . . ."

"That's because you're tired," I said, which was a mistake. For four-year-olds, they were really good at explaining what "tired" was and why they didn't have it.

When I finally had them settled into bed, I tried to leave . . .

"Don't go, Lucía!" screamed Greta. "What if something realizes I'm food and eats me!"

"I bet you don't taste very good," I said.

Greta stared at me with an open mouth, shocked and offended. "I do too taste very good. I taste like cookies!"

I couldn't argue with that.

In the end, I moved their pillows and blankets onto the floor and lay between them. They snuggled up into me like kittens with a mama cat.

"You're a good tuckler," said Henna. "You know how to snuckle."

"Nice Lucía," said Greta, patting my head. "Good girl, Lucía. You get a cookie."

I was afraid to say it. "There aren't any more cookies."

"There are always more cookies," Henna whispered.

I heard a crunch. Where had that one been stashed, in her underwear? She offered me half of it. I said no thanks.

Henna kept chewing and wiggling. Greta went still, her head resting on my shoulder.

"Santa Claus is not evil," she sang under her breath. "He will try not to kill you when he comes into your hoooooouse . . ."

I must have dozed off because the window was dark when I woke back up. Greta and Henna were both snoozing beside me.

I carefully scooted out from between them and tiptoed back into the kitchen. I was cleaning up the dinner dishes when Mrs. Grady came through the front door.

"How'd it go?" she asked, looking around as if

expecting to see the girls. Or perhaps a fire or flood.

"Um ... pretty good," I said, rubbing my eyes. "You know, they've got a lot of energy. But I guess they worked it all out because they're asleep now—"

"They're asleep?" she said.

She ran down the hallway and peeked in the room. She wandered back, her face all dreamy.

"They're asleep! They're actually asleep. Usually when I have a sitter, the most I can hope for is that everyone survives and property damage is minimal."

She handed me some bills, three times my usual fee.

"We'd love to have you back," she said with a super-cheery-hopeful smile. "Anytime!"

"I ... I'll think about it." We headed toward the door, passing the glass cookie jar. "Sorry about—" *letting the girls eat all the cookies,* I started to say. But I could see the jar was nearly full. "How did that happen?" I blurted out.

Mrs. Grady smiled. "There are always more cookies," she said.

Goose bumps.

Dear Bella and Rover (Again)

By Deborah Underwood

Dear . . . Bella . . . and . . . Rover,
I . . . am . . . a . . . snail. I . . . move . . . slowly. When . . .
my . . . insect . . . friends . . . and . . . I . . . race . . . I . . .
always . . . lose. How . . . can . . . I . . . be . . . faster?
Love . . .
Olivia

Dear Olivia,

*Here's the thing: snails are not exactly built for speed.
But there are a lot of cool things about YOU that your
insect friends can only dream of! Right, Rover?*

**You bet! Snails have great sturdy shells! If it starts
raining pebbles . . .**

Raining pebbles?

You never know! If it starts raining pebbles, your insect friends will be in trouble, but you can just pull yourself into your shell and you'll be safe! And the best part is that you leave beautiful shimmering rainbow trails wherever you go! I wish I could leave rainbow trails when I go for a walk! Instead, I leave poo—

Never mind! Olivia, Rover is absolutely right. Why not focus on the things that make YOU amazing? And instead of racing with your friends, find something that you're all good at to do when you're together. For instance, Rover is good at ripping up tennis balls, but I'm not.

And Bella is good at clawing her way up the window screen, but I'm not.

But there's one thing we both love and we're both great at . . .

  TAKING NAPS!
  And it's nap time right now. Good luck, Olivia!

Love,
Bella and **Rover**

Can We Talk About Whiskers?

By Jennifer L. Holm, art by Matthew Holm

Everyone thinks that the brand of shoes you wear or the sport you play is what's important in middle school. But the truth is that it all comes down to whiskers.

I should know.

My name is Babymouse.

And I have the worst whiskers in the entire world.

My whiskers have always been crazy. I've tried just about every whisker-straightening treatment that exists. Leave-in conditioner. Gel. Mousse.

This morning I decided to try something different: flat-ironing. The flat iron seemed pretty easy to use. The first whisker I ironed turned out great. It was so easy that I decided to turn up the heat to the top setting to get the rest of them as straight as possible. Unfortunately, I turned up the setting *too* high and ended up with . . . *toasted whiskers.*

Typical.

When I got to school, I kept my head down and went straight to my locker. I was wearing a filmy scarf to hide my burnt whiskers. Naturally, my locker didn't open on the first try. Locker had a mind of its own. And it didn't like me one bit.

I was struggling to open up the metal beast when I saw her: Felicia Furrypaws.

AKA the Queen of Perfect Whiskers.

Felicia was the most popular girl in school. She always had two or three girls trailing after her like fans.

"Your whiskers look fabulous, Felicia," one of the other girls said.

"They're so shiny!" another observed.

"And straight!" the third added.

"I got whisker extensions," Felicia announced to the admiring group.

"Whisker extensions?" I blurted out.

Felicia looked at me and raised one perfect eyebrow. "Yes, they're the latest. Everybody's getting them."

I guess *everybody* didn't include *me* because I hadn't even heard about them.

"Picture Day is next week. I want to look good," Felicia said.

Picture Day? My stomach fell.

Then Felicia said, "By the way, Babymouse. I love your scarf. Can I try it on?"

"I—" I started to say.

"Thanks!" she interrupted and whipped it off, revealing my sad whiskers.

"Oh," she said, "that's an interesting look, Babymouse."

Then she and the girls walked away, laughing.

Le sigh.

Wilson came up to my locker a moment later.

"Hey, Babymouse," he said.

"Hi, Wilson."

Wilson had been my best friend forever. Everybody needed a weaselly best friend, in my opinion.

"Want to go to the movies on Friday night? There's a werewolf movie playing."

"Sure," I said.

When I got home from school, I went straight to my mother.

"Picture Day is next week," I told her. "Can I get whisker extensions?"

She shook her head. "They're very expensive, Babymouse. Each whisker is one hundred dollars."

One hundred dollars a whisker? Talk about whisker robbery!

"I'm sorry, Babymouse," she said.

What was I going to do?

* * *

Wilson and I sat in the dark theater and watched werewolves roar across the screen.

I loved horror movies because the monsters were obvious. Vampires had fangs, and werewolves had claws, and zombies had rotting flesh. It was harder to figure out who the monsters were in real life.

After the movie, we grabbed a cupcake.

"What did you think?" Wilson asked.

"It was pretty good," I said.

"The werewolves had great makeup!" Wilson en-thused. "They looked totally real."

"That's it!" I exclaimed.

Wilson gave me a puzzled look. "Huh?"

I pointed to my face. "I want to get whisker exten-sions, but they're too expensive. We can do it with monster makeup!"

"I don't know, Babymouse. It's pretty hard . . ."

Hard was walking around with singed whiskers.

This was easy.

* * *

We spent the rest of the weekend trying to figure out how to create straight whiskers with stage makeup. It took a ~~little~~ lot of trial and error.

But it all paid off, because when I walked into school on Monday morning I had perfect, straight whiskers. Heads turned left and right as I walked down the hallway to my locker. It was time for pictures!

I gave my whiskers a final check in the locker, and then the bell rang.

And then Felicia walked up.

"Nice whiskers, Babymouse!" Felicia said, adding with a sly smile, "Or should I say *whisker*?"

Typical.

Brown Girl Pop Quiz: All of the Above

By Mitali Perkins

1. Why is Indian food so spicy?

   a. Sweating while eating means you're burning calories. At least that's what my sister says when she gets seconds of Mom's lamb curry. Which makes me go for thirds.

   b. Spicy food relaxes the body. Who needs to take a smartphone into the bathroom for an hour?

   c. Chop up a chili pepper and add it to your next tuna fish sandwich. Yum, right? I rest my case.

   d. All of the above.

2. Why do I have to take off my shoes when I visit?

a. All of Asia does that to keep dirt outside where it belongs. And to welcome people with clean feet inside, where we belong. Come in, good to see you, have some tea, but don't bring flattened cow dung into our living room, thank you very much.

b. You just stepped in dog dung. My bad—my turn to clean up after Pohdoo. Thanks for helping.

c. So your socks can clean the kitchen floor. My turn to sweep, too.

d. All of the above.

3. Are all Indian American kids nerds?

a. I sure hope my teachers think so. Maybe they'll subconsciously grade me higher. Maybe they'll tell me all homework assignments are optional. Maybe the principal will suggest to my parents that attendance in classes is optional. A South Asian genius like me should be free to pursue academic passions at home. In my pajamas.

b. Nope. Only the ones who win the National Spelling Bee.

c. Some of us are jocks. Want to take me on in tennis?

d. All of the above.

4. Do you speak Indian?

a. Only a few cuss words I can't really use. Dadu, our grandfather, taught me the *real* words for private body parts during a boring dinner party. Turns out Dad named Pohdoo after the part our dog likes to sniff when people visit.

b. Do you speak American? There's no language called Indian. My parents speak Bengali, which is one of the 122 or so languages in India. Dadu knows how to swear in Hindi, Marathi, Urdu, and Oriya.

c. I don't speak Hindu, either. That's a religion, not a language. The national language of India is Hindi. Do people speak Jewish? How do you say Pohdoo in Hebrew anyway?

d. All of the above.

5. Why is your mother wearing a red dot on her forehead?

   a. I think it has something to do with the third eye of Shiva. Let's ask the third eye of Google.

   b. These days, Indian women wear dots or bindis on their foreheads like makeup, to match lipstick and eye shadow.

   c. It's a good way to hide a big zit.

   d. All of the above.

6. Why is there so much singing and dancing in Indian movies?

   a. To give viewers a chance to pee without missing too much of the plot.

   b. The real question is this: why isn't there more singing and dancing in American movies? I can't think of a Hollywood flick that wouldn't be better if they put in a good song and dance number. Think of Jedi knights doing a choreographed number after the Death Star explodes, for example.

c. Wouldn't you rather watch actors sing and dance for five minutes than watch them kiss for five minutes? Thank you, Bollywood censors.

d. All of the above.

7. Are your parents going to arrange your marriage?

a. Chill. I'm only in sixth grade. Ask me again once I'm out of college.

b. By then, Mom and Dad will be exhausted. My sister and the dudes she dates—like the barefoot vegan training to be a tattoo artist, now that he's out of jail—are doing a great job of breaking down the parents.

c. Is the Internet going to arrange your marriage? Because it's way more stupid than my parents.

d. All of the above.

8. Don't you love it when Coach Owens has us do yoga in PE?

a. Touchy subject. My ancestors did not give me the yoga gene. These limbs do not twist into pretzels.

b. When I bend down, my toes are soooooo far away. *waves to toes*

c. My tree pose is more of a deforestation pose. Namaste yourself, Coach. *falls over*

d. All of the above.

9. **Have you ever worn a sari?**

a. Yes. But remind me to use safety pins next time. That whole tucking and folding thing didn't work quite right. I was sari to see my granny panties revealed in public. Guess it was better than exposing my pohdoo.

b. Yes. And I felt beautiful.

c. Yes. It's fun making grandmothers cry. *For joy!* Sheesh. I'm not a monster.

d. All of the above.

10. **Do you think of yourself as Indian or American?**

a. Our family roots for Team Red, White, and Blue in the Olympics, but we also cheer like crazy when the Indian athletes march in carrying that beautiful orange and green and white flag.

b. Both.

c. Neither.

d. All of the above.

Over and Out

By Lisa Graff

"Now that Deirdre's sixteen she thinks other people don't need to use the bathroom. Over." Riley released the button on her walkie-talkie and waited for her best friend to respond from his apartment five floors below. Nothing. She pressed the button again. "Got your ears on, Simon? Over." Riley wriggled onto her belly to peer through the gap below the bathroom door. She could see her sister's legs at the sink. "She's been in there forever. Over."

At last Simon's voice squawked over the walkie. "Just tell her you have to pee," he said. "Over and out. Or is it 'Mayday'? I'm coming up now to play Yahtzee."

"You say 'Over' when you're done talking," Riley informed Simon for the millionth time. "'Mayday' is for serious trouble, like a boat sinking. 'Over and out' is when you're finished talking for good. And I need to do more than pee. Over."

"I did not need to know that. Over."

That's when the door was whipped open. "Riley Gershwin!" Deirdre hollered. "Stop spying on me!"

"I wasn't spying," Riley lied, rolling to her feet. "I was checking if you wanted to play Yahtzee. Matthew and Logan might play, too." Matthew and Logan were Simon's older brothers. Matthew was thirteen and always working on bizarre inventions, and Logan was sixteen like Deirdre but not nearly as annoying.

"No way those two are playing Yahtzee," Deirdre said. She squeezed some goop from a tube into her hand.

"How do you know?" Riley challenged.

"Because." Deirdre ran the goop through her hair. "They're not ten."

Deirdre had once been an actual fun human being, before she started spending all her time texting and hogging the bathroom. Last summer she'd joined Riley and Simon in a weeklong Yahtzee marathon, and when she'd scored three Yahtzees in a single game, her touchdown dance had put the Giants' wide receiver to shame. Now she looked at Riley like a cockroach whose guts had squished all over her shoe.

Maybe turning sixteen was like getting bitten by a werewolf. Only instead of growing fangs and howling, you grew unbearably boring.

"I'm leaving," Deirdre said. "Mom and Dad know where I'll be."

"Don't lock the front door," Riley told her sister. "Simon's coming up."

Deirdre jerked her head toward the towel rack beside the toilet. "Don't let your little friend ogle my bra," she replied.

Riley took in the neon pink bra that hung from the towel rack. "Can't you wash your underwear in the laundry room like a normal person?" she asked.

"Bras are delicate," Deirdre answered. "They need to be hand-washed and air-dried. You'll understand when you grow boobs."

Riley's eyeballs were boiling in their sockets as Deirdre made her way across the dining room. "Maybe I'll just flush your bra down the toilet!" she hollered.

"Lay one finger on that bra," Deirdre snapped back, "and I'll *murder* you." And with that, she slammed shut the apartment door behind her.

Riley squeezed past the towel rack that held her sister's precious bra and unbuttoned her shorts. She plopped her bare butt down on the toilet and began her business, hoping that when she turned sixteen, she'd have the sense not to worry about things like ugly pink br—

Riley squinted at the towel rack, just inches from her shoulder.

Deirdre's bra was missing.

Panic rose in Riley's throat as she rose to her feet,

yanking up her shorts. Slowly she turned.

Floating inside the toilet was her sister's neon pink bra. Riley must have knocked it off the towel rack before she sat down. But worse than that—worse than anything Riley had done in her entire life—was what had come after.

Riley Gershwin had *pooped* on her sister's *bra*.

"*Simon?*" Riley called, whipping open the bathroom door. "Are you here yet? I need help!"

No Simon. Riley turned back to the toilet and reached for the plunger beside the tank. Her only option was to fish out the bra and wash it and hang it back on the towel rack before Deirdre noticed it was missing. But as she reached, Riley bumped the toilet handle, and with a violent spurt of water the bra began to twist inside the bowl. The poop was sucked down, and the bra followed close behind. "Give me that!" Riley screeched, snagging one strap with the plunger handle. As the toilet let out its final *slurp!* Riley yanked the bra out—sending it soaring over her shoulder, out the bathroom door, speckling everything in its path with toilet water.

Simon was standing just beside the dining room table when Riley turned. The bra swinging from the chandelier above him scattered eerie shadows across the walls.

"Is this the kind of thing where you'd say 'Mayday'?" he asked. Then, noticing the scowl on Riley's face, he added, "Over."

*　*　*

"I thought Deirdre told you this . . . *thing* had to be hand-washed," Simon said as the elevator lurched toward the basement laundry room. The bra dripped from a pair of kitchen tongs in his outstretched hand.

Riley hoisted the bottle of laundry detergent further into her armpit. "No way am I hand-washing something that's been pooped on," she said, then added, "Hi, Mrs. Applebaum!" when their third-floor neighbor entered the elevator with her yappy dog.

"Nugget, stop that," Mrs. Applebaum told the dog, without looking up from her phone. Nugget was sniffing at the soiled bra.

Simon lifted the tongs a little higher.

When the doors opened to the lobby, Mrs. Applebaum stepped out, and Riley told her, "Have a lovely day!" And then Riley spotted Simon's oldest brother, Logan, across the lobby floor by the coffee kiosk. "Does Logan drink *coffee* now?" she asked Simon, leaning to see around a giant pillar.

Mrs. Applebaum was yanking at Nugget's leash, her eyes still on her phone. "Come, boy!"

Simon shifted to see around the pillar, too. "Logan's

with a *girl*," he exclaimed. And then: "Nugget, *no!*"

Riley dumped the detergent bottle on the ground, but it was too late. Nugget had snapped up the bra in his sharp doggy teeth and was trying to snatch it away from Simon.

Mrs. Applebaum finally looked up from her phone. "Is that a *bra*?" she screeched.

Thinking fast, Riley dug a half-empty packet of M&M's from her pocket and flung it out the elevator door. Nugget released the bra and lunged for the chocolate, sending Mrs. Applebaum scurrying after him. Riley pounded the CLOSE button as Mrs. Applebaum shouted, *"Hooligans!"*

"Do you think my brother was on a *date*?" Simon asked as the elevator shook back to life.

Riley plucked the bra off the elevator floor. It was riddled with chew marks and dog drool. Clearly she needed a new plan. Clearly her problems had gotten a little too big for mere washing machines. "I think," she said, pressing the button to return to her own floor, "that I'm about to get murdered."

*　　*　　*

It turns out that when a dog tries to eat a bra, it can't be fixed with wood glue.

"That's *it!*" Riley declared, snatching up the sticky

bra between a pair of oven mitts and bolting out of her apartment, down the long hallway. Simon hustled to keep pace.

"But Deirdre will notice it's missing," he said when they reached the garbage chute.

"She'll never be able to prove I'm the one who took it." Riley tugged open the chute's small square door and stuffed the bra inside, waiting for the sweet sound of the bra landing on soggy garbage in the basement below.

Instead, she heard a voice, tinny but familiar, echoing up from the darkness. *"Whoa."* It was Simon's middle brother, Matthew. *"Is this a BRA?"* he said.

*   *   *

A tennis racket covered in glue traps—that was Matthew's latest invention. He'd been hoping, he explained, to catch some "incriminating documents" from the businessman in their building's penthouse, but on his very first test run, he'd snagged something else entirely.

"Is it Deirdre's?" Matthew asked them, tossing the neon pink underwear from hand to hand.

"We found it in the park," Riley told him. "What are you gonna do with it?"

"I'm going to hang it out the window like a flag," Matthew said. "Make everyone on Fulton Street say the pledge of allegiance."

Riley couldn't even begin to imagine how mortified her sister would be at that. A person might as well scream, *"HEY, EVERYONE! THAT'S MY UNDER-WEAR!"*

"I'll pay you for it," Riley told Matthew. "One hundred and sixty bucks."

Matthew let out a whistle. "You just bought yourself a bra," he said.

As they skittered off to fetch the money, Riley told Simon, "Okay, so I don't actually have one hundred and sixty dollars." Sixteen, that's what she had: a ten, a five, and a one—her birthday money from Bubbe Ruth, minus four dollars she'd spent on M&M's. "But I'll draw zeros on all the bills, and while Matthew's yelling at me for cheating him, you'll grab the bra and make a run for it. Meet me at the carousel in Battery Park. We can live off the land, right?"

"No way am I touching *underwear* that someone *pooped* on," Simon argued.

"When Deirdre murders me," Riley reminded him, "you'll have no one to play Yahtzee with."

And Simon could hardly argue with that.

* * *

Simon did manage to grab the bra while Riley was fighting with Matthew, but he only got as far as his own kitchen.

"Dad!" Riley heard him call. "Mom! Didn't expect to see you here. Hey, Bill and Wanda!" Riley gulped. Bill and Wanda were *her* parents. "Want to hear a knock knock joke?"

Riley raced to the kitchen, with Matthew on her heels.

"Why did the broccoli cross the road?" Simon asked the crowd of parents.

Simon's dad made his way to the sink. "Broccoli?" he asked. Riley didn't see the bra anywhere. She made bug-eyes at Simon, but he was too focused on his terrible joke-telling to notice.

"Be-*cause*," he went on, "it was in a *casserole*! Get it? Cass-a-*roll*? Like the broccoli's in a casserole car?" Silence. "Okay, I'll work on it."

Riley only barely noticed that Simon's dad was running water in the sink.

Only barely paid attention when he flicked on the disposal.

"What are you guys doing here?" she asked her parents.

Riley's father winked at her. "Just wanted to see how Deirdre's date went."

"Deirdre's on a *date*?" Riley squealed.

Her mother waved a dismissive hand. "Oh, it's not really a date," she said. "Just two kids drinking decaf."

At the sink, Simon's dad turned off the disposal.

"What the heck is in here?" he asked, stuffing his hand inside the sink.

At the counter, Riley's best friend had turned a putrid shade of green. And soon Riley knew why.

When Simon's father pulled his arm from the sink with a sickening *schloooook!* there was something dangling from the end of his index finger.

Something pink.

Something ripped, and wet, too.

It had been pooped on, chewed up, glued together, stuffed down a garbage chute, stuck to a tennis racket, and run through a garbage disposal.

But it was still, somehow, unmistakably, a bra.

Riley groaned. Matthew hooted. Simon grew even more broccoli-green. "Oh, my," declared Riley's dad.

And that was precisely when Deirdre walked through the door, hand in hand with Logan.

Riley realized two things then, both at once.

The first thing was that her sister was not a werewolf. Gazing dreamily as she was at the side of Logan's face, Deirdre looked *happy*. Even happier than she had when she'd scored that third Yahtzee. It was a nice look for her. Very unwerewolfy.

The second thing Riley realized was that when Deirdre and Logan turned—in one split second, they were about to do it—they would see the bra. And Logan would know just from the expression on Deirdre's face that it was hers, and Deirdre wouldn't look so happy anymore. Riley wouldn't even care when she got murdered after that, because she'd deserve it for mortifying her unwerewolf sister so badly.

And so, just as Deirdre and Logan turned toward the bra, Riley did the only thing she could think to do.

"HEY, EVERYONE!" she hollered. "THAT'S MY UNDERWEAR!" And then she snatched the bra right out of Simon's father's hand and dashed out the door, down the hall, and up five flights to her own apartment. When she got there, she flushed the bra down the toilet.

It went right down.

Riley plopped herself on her bed and tugged her walkie-talkie out of her pocket. She wanted to ask Simon what had happened after she'd left. She wanted to ask if he thought Deirdre would ever speak to her again. But she didn't have the heart to press the button.

*   *   *

Riley had been lying on her bed for a good forty minutes when the walkie squawked to life beside her.

"You push that one," came Simon's voice from the other end. "And you say, 'Over,' or something."

"Are you *ever* going to learn how to use this thing?" Riley asked, snatching up the walkie. "Over."

But it wasn't Simon who answered her.

"Riley?"

It was Deirdre.

Riley sat up on her bed. "Yeah?" she said into the walkie. "Over."

There was a pause, and then another squawk.

"Want to play Yahtzee?" Deirdre asked.

Just then, Riley felt a bit like a werewolf who had seen a full moon for the first time—like the world was a wonderful place, brighter than she'd ever imagined. "Sure," she told her sister. And then she smiled. "Over and out."

Doodle
by
Amy Ignatow

In 2009 Dr. Jackie Andrade, Professor of Psychology at the University of Plymouth, published a study entitled, "What Does Doodling do?"

She had a group of people listen to a long, boring phone message. Half of the people were encouraged to doodle, and the other half were not.

Afterward the participants were asked to recall details from the message. The people who doodled remembered far more details than the ones who didn't.

So the next time that you need to focus on what someone is saying, doodle. If anyone thinks you aren't paying attention, just tell them about the study.

Is that supposed to be me?

Uh...did you know that in 2009 Dr. Jackie Andrade, Professor of Psychology at the University of Plymouth...

You have a monster eating my head.

I swear, I'm totally paying attention.

Fleamail Pawed-cast

By Deborah Underwood

Good morning! I'm Bella...

And I'm Rover.

Welcome to Bella and Rover's first-ever call-in pawed-cast!

Who do we have on the line with us today?

I'm Teeny.

I'm Tiny.

We are fighting fish and we fight all the time.

No we don't.

Yes we do. And we want to stop.

No we don't.

Yes we do.

No we don't . . . actually, we do. It's exhausting.

Can you help us?

Hi! Bella here. I understand. Fighting can be quite draining. You should—

Hey. Why is it always Bella and Rover? Why not Rover and Bella?

Because I'm a cat.

Why should cats be first?

Okay. It's alphabetical. B comes before R.

That's not fair!

Yes it is!

No it isn't!

Yes it is!

Wow. Teeny, do we sound like that when we fight?

They're ridiculous! I don't want to be ridiculous!

Me neither. Hey—want to swim over and check out the castle?

Sure. Friends?

Friends!

Yes it is!

No it isn't! . . . have they hung up yet?

Yup. High-five-paws! We rock!

Hey. Why *is* your name always first?

That's all we have time for today. Tune in next week to Bella and **Rover!**

Rover *and Bella.*

Bella and **Rover.**

How to Play
Imaginary Games

By Leila Sales

How to Play Disney Princesses

Necessary materials:

- A large bed.

Game setup: Stand on the end of the large bed.

Start play by pricking your finger on a spindle, or taking a bite of a poisoned apple—one or the other, depending on your hair color.

Step two: Faint backward onto the bed as dramatically as possible.

Repeat steps one and two indefinitely.

How to Determine the Winner of This Game: The winner is you, unless you break your parents' bed, in which case the winner is Maleficent.

How to Play Orphanage

Necessary materials:

- A book of baby names.

- Paper and pencil.
- Bread and water.

Game setup: Populate your orphanage by going through the baby name book and selecting as many names as you want. An orphan named Annie is obviously a good choice. You could also have identical triplet orphans named Cora, Coral, and Corinne. Or identical quintuplet orphans named Larissa, Clarissa, Marissa, Melissa, and Alyssa. These are just examples. Write down all your orphans' names so you don't forget them. Draw small portraits of each of them, making sure they all have sad eyes. Some may also have courage evident in their faces. Those are the ones who still pathetically cling to dreams of a better life.

Start play by pretending to be all the orphans. Not all at once—that would be weird. Alternate among them. Do some thankless chores assigned to you by the cruel matron, who threatens to take away the one memento your parents left you should you disobey. Try to stage an escape: hide in your closet until the matron has stepped outside for a cigarette (obviously Matron is a smoker), then run as though your life depends on it.

Step two: When it's lunchtime at the orphanage, ask your parents to give you a plate of bread and a glass of water. This is all you get to eat. Even if they offer you Oreos or ants on a log. Say no. SAY NO. THAT IS THE

RULE OF THE GAME. ARE WE PLAYING THIS GAME, OR ARE WE JUST HANGING OUT AND EATING SNACKS?

The game ends when all the orphans die from consumption.

How to Determine the Winner of This Game: Anyone left alive is the winner.

How to Play Capture

Necessary materials:

- A number of strawberry baskets linked together with yarn.
- A bunch of small, vulnerable-looking things, like plastic ponies.
- A dark evil inside of you.

Start play by having your small, vulnerable items hanging out and enjoying their day. Maybe they are swimming in the pool of your cat's water bowl, or maybe they are getting their hair braided at the beauty salon in your bathroom. Just make sure you establish that it is a great, relaxing day to belong to a community of small, vulnerable things. What could ever go wrong in such a dreamland?

Step two: The Bad Guy arrives. You don't need an actual tangible Bad Guy. Like, if you have a giant evil-looking stuffed animal, that's great, but otherwise the

Bad Guy can just be an unseen and overpowering force. The Bad Guy is you, technically speaking, but don't think too hard about that because that is very existential.

The Bad Guy brings with him a monorail bound for one destination only: prison camp. The monorail is a long chain of strawberry baskets, each of which is perfectly sized for holding one family of plastic objects. Load them all in. They cannot bring their beauty salon supplies with them. There is no swimming pool where they are going.

Drag them down the hall in the strawberry basket train. Have them weep audibly. Bonus move: Some of them try to stage an escape. It doesn't work, of course. You can't escape the Bad Guy. These foolhardy plastic souls go tumbling down the stairs to the foyer, where hours later your father will step on them with bare feet and yell at you.

Stop play when the train reaches its prison camp destination: your mother's study. Everyone is crowded into little jail cells on your mother's bookcase. Life as they knew it is now over. Abandon them, just as they have abandoned all hope. Go play with something else. Let your mother clean them up later.

How to Determine the Winner of This Game: There are no winners.

Great Expectations

By Christine Mari Inzer

A Public Service Announcement About Your Period from Sarah T. Wrigley, Age 12¾

By Libba Bray

Dear Friends,

Sarah T. Wrigley here, Period Protocol Expert of Harry Truman Middle School. Today I'm going to talk to you about your period.

Maybe you've just started your period. Maybe you're still a ways off and wondering what all the fuss is about. Maybe you're not sure who to talk to about it. Or maybe you're afraid people will act all weird and freak you out if you *do* talk about it. (Oh, hi, Mom!)

Well, I started my period three months ago, so I am practically an *expert* on the subject. Sure, I suppose I could tell you about how your body works and all that stuff. But that's what the school nurse and those little movies they make you watch are for. Me? I'm here to help with the stuff *nobody* tells you. Like what happens if Caleb Cooper pours apple juice all over your tampon art project. Think of me as your Period President and this is my Period Public Service Announcement.

You're welcome.

1. Your Grown-Ups Might Get Weird.

Prepare yourselves: When you get your first period, your grown-ups get super weird.

Take my mom, for example. When I told her I'd started (which I knew because there was a streak of blood in my new undies—ugh, thanks, universe. Why not the old undies?), she gave me a hug like we were in one of those TV commercials where people are so super happy that their allergies are fixed that they can't stop smiling while walking the dog.

Then she handed me an envelope. Was it a fro-yo gift card? Was it money? Money! Like a period allowance! Side note: Friends, when I am the President of Periods, I am so establishing a first-period cash fund—fifty bucks to spend any way you want. And free frozen yogurt.

Spoiler alert: It was a greeting card. On the front, there was a glittery unicorn prancing under a shiny rainbow that spelled out "Congratulations!" I spent *ten whole minutes* trying to figure out what unicorns and rainbows had to do with getting your period. Let me save you the trouble: There is no connection that I can see. My mom needs professional help.

I said, "Mom. Why is there a sparkly, prancing unicorn on my weird period greeting card? Is it like a My Little Pony thing? Is the glitter unicorn the official mascot of our periods now? Because I am seriously freaked out by this. Look at its eyes, Mom. They aren't right." Seriously, it had the eyes of a killer. I had to bury that card in my sock drawer.

Mom got weepy. "I just wanted to mark this passage. You're a woman now, honey."

I performed some anti-hug maneuvers. "No, Mom. I'm not. I'm, like, *twelve and a half*? I can't even drive. You won't even let me watch *Super Housewives*."

"That show is inappropriate for a seventh grader," Mom said.

"I'm pretty sure they have lots of periods on that show. It would be educational," I tried.

BIG MISTAKE!

I did NOT get to watch *Super Housewives*. Instead, Mom made me watch a period-explaining YouTube video while my little brother ran back and forth shouting, "Fallopian tubes! Ovaries! Uterus!" which, PS, he was still shouting when we went to the grocery store later.

I am not okay with that.

So be ready: Tell your grown-ups the only thing you need to mark your special day is money. And do NOT ask if you can see *Super Housewives* or you'll end up watching period videos with your little brother. You've been warned.

2. Tampons Are Not Building Blocks. Pads Are Not Flower Arrangements.

In second grade, my friend Chloe thought that tampons were some kind of new soft building blocks. For her art project, she built an entire replica of the Acropolis from a box of tampons she found under the sink in her mom's bathroom. All those Greek columns? Tampons.

It was pretty rad. Not as rad as our teacher Mrs. Jackson's face as she tried to figure out what to say besides, "Ummm ... wow."

That's when Caleb Cooper poured his apple juice all over it to see what would happen. He has serious impulse issues. Honestly, he should be barred from all liquids. Turns out tampons really are super absorbent! Chloe's Acropolis ballooned into a little tampon sausage house. You couldn't even see the door anymore. I felt bad for the Fisher Price Little People trapped inside. Their eyes showed real fear, like, "Wait a minute! This is so not the Happy Times Ice Cream Shoppe we were promised!" We had to use the Jaws of Life (Mrs. Jackson's safety scissors) to cut them out. I'm pretty sure those Little People still have toy nightmares.

But I can understand why Chloe made her mistake.

Because tampons and maxi-/mini-pads come in pastel boxes that are covered in hearts or flowers or stars. It's like the unicorn all over again: What do our periods have to do with Valentine's Day and a florist's shop?

When I am the President of Periods, I'm going to design cool boxes: Skulls. Jet Packs. Wonder Woman. Bikes. Maybe some polar bears because I really love polar bears. Pizza. An octopus wearing a monocle. I mean, if you could choose between a weird pastel flower or an octopus wearing a monocle, which would you choose? Please. That's not even a question.

3. Own It!

Sometimes, people try to make you feel embarrassed about having your period. Like it's an FBI-level secret covered in girl cooties. That's bananapants! Having your period's just a natural part of growing up. Like, when boys' voices get deeper, nobody says to them, "Psst! Boys: you might want to keep this private."

We've been having periods for, like, a GAJILLION YEARS. Get over it.

Now let me tell you about Alana Robinson. Last year, when she got her period, she formed a club with her three best friends called The Period Posse. One week out of the month, they wear these cool red satin jackets, and when the four of them walk down the hall of Harry Truman Middle School like a band of menstruating superheroes? I'm talking wind-machine awesome. You can absolutely start a club or make jackets or come up with your own dance moves—"We call this move 'The Flow'!" Make it a party if you want. Own it.

4. Try Giving Your Period a Nickname.

Did you know there are lots of fun nicknames for having your period? Aunt Flo. The Red Baron. Crimson tide. That time of the month. Riding the bus. Having a visitor. Peddling the unicycle. The Dot. Punctuation time. It's a girl week. Hosting the Uterus Dance Club. Paddling the canoe. Old Faithful. I call mine Rhiannon. Like, "Oh, I'm hanging out with Rhiannon this week." Like I've got a rock star cousin who comes to visit once a month. You can call yours anything you want. Sarah T. Wrigley, for example. I would be honored to be the nickname of your monthly.

5. Accidents Will Happen.

What happens if you bleed through your jeans? Well, you *could* punch your fist in the air and say, "That's right! I got my period. LIKE A BOSS! I'm outta here. Later, suckers," on your way to the bathroom. You could cause a distraction—"OMG, is that K-pop sensation Too Much Love out on the lawn of our school?"—while you make a run for it. Or you could keep a sweater with you to wrap around your waist. You think Alana Robinson came up with red satin jackets on a whim? Nope. That was a genius plan. I want to grow up to be Alana Robinson. Maybe she can be my VP of Periods.

5. Don't Worry.

Look, maybe you've already started. Maybe your friends have all hopped the pink bus and you're afraid you won't get to board. Or maybe there's a Megan Wilson at your school who likes to brag-moan, "Oh my gosh, y'all, I am soooo crampy!" like having your period is an Olympic sport and she's going for the gold. Nobody's impressed, Megan. Also, all that "Oh, you're a woman now?" *Whatever, part two.*

(Confession: From time to time, I still drag out my old Barbies because I miss them. Last week, Barbie got her period. Skipper tried to hug her. Barbie said no. Then she rode her new bike.)

As your period guru, I can promise you—it's all good.

Except for glitter unicorns. That's just messed up, Mom.

Wishing you the best period ever!

Sincerely,

Your Period President,

Sarah T. Wrigley, Age 12 ¾

The Smart Girl's Guide to the Chinese Zodiac

By Lenore Look

In China, individual birth dates are not as important as the year in which you were born. And if you want to know someone's age, you don't ask how old they are, but the animal sign in which they were born.

The Chinese zodiac is a twelve-year-cycle based on the lunar calendar, where each year is represented by a different animal. Humans are said to possess the characteristics of the animals under which they are born, and their success in life depends on how well they manage their animal natures.

Having problems with a parent, sibling, friend, or romantic interest? Want to know your strengths and weaknesses? The amazing Chinese zodiac explains it all!

* * *

Find Your Animal Year!

RAT	1960	1972	1984	1996	2008	2020
OX	1961	1973	1985	1997	2009	2021
TIGER	1962	1974	1986	1998	2010	2022
RABBIT	1963	1975	1987	1999	2011	2023
DRAGON	1964	1976	1988	2000	2012	2024
SNAKE	1965	1977	1989	2001	2013	2025
HORSE	1966	1978	1990	2002	2014	2026
GOAT	1967	1979	1991	2003	2015	2027
MONKEY	1968	1980	1992	2004	2016	2028
ROOSTER	1969	1981	1993	2005	2017	2029
DOG	1970	1982	1994	2006	2018	2030
PIG	1971	1983	1995	2007	2019	2031

RAT

Legend has it that when the Buddha was dying, he summoned all the animals to his side, but only twelve came. The Buddha was cool with that because paper hadn't been invented yet, and it took him forever to chisel on his tablet the names of the animals in the order of their arrival. The Ox ran the fastest, but the Rat was the cleverest. He jumped on Ox's back to cross a river, then hopped to the other side and ran ahead. Never underestimate the power and ability of the little guy!

Lucky traits: Funny. Clever. Loyal friend. Generous. A cute nose, too!

Unlucky traits: Long tail. Short fuse. Overly critical.

Lucky car: Maserati.

Lucky crushes: Dragon or Monkey. If you have any doubt, stay with your own kind—moles, mice, bats, small sized rabbits.

Fatal Attractions: Horse. Eagles. Falcons. Owls. Buzzards.

Unlucky sports: Soccer. Lacrosse. Field hockey. Anything that requires running across an open field (see Fatal Attractions). Marathons are especially lethal. Bowling is a bad idea.

Famous Rats: Wolfgang Amadeus Molezart, Leo Volestoy, John Cage, T. Squirrel Eliot.

OX/BULL/COW

You are a visionary, and determination is your middle name. People like to follow you.

Lucky traits: Inspiring. Charismatic. Dependable.

Unlucky traits: Conservative. Rule follower. Stubborn. Hot-tempered.

Lucky hairstyle: Uncombed. Go for the natural, roll-off-the-field look. You're gorgeous just the way you are!

Lucky outfit to wear on a date: A muumuu.

Unlucky bling: Anything loud that hangs around your neck.

Unlucky crushes: The Goat will get your goat. Every time.

Should you ask your crush out? Only when you're in a good mood. How would *you* like to be approached by a mad Bull?

Unlucky careers: Inventory control manager in a china shop. Red flag chaser consultant (temp job) in Barcelona.

Extremely unlucky sport: Bullfighting (see temp job in Barcelona).

Famous Bovines: Aroastotle, Johann Sebastian Bull, Dante Alidairy, Moogaret Thatcher.

TIGER

RRRRRrrrr! Hello Kitty you are not. You are the empress of all the animals.

Lucky traits: Powerful. Courageous. Ambitious.

Unlucky traits: Moody. Rebellious. Unpredictable. Always dominant. Tigers are not good followers.

Lucky nail color: Orange You Wild?

Unlucky outfit for a date: Last night's dinner. Meat is *not* a fashion statement.

Unlucky crushes: You get so many mixed signals from Monkey. Best to avoid.

Should you ask your crush out? Never. There is only one response when a Tiger approaches!

Lucky careers: Military ambush specialist. Ninja. Assassin.

Unlucky careers: Tiger balm. Rug.

Famous Tigers: Ludwig van Bengaloven, Queen Elizabite II, Ho Chi Mean, Sun Catsen, Marilyn Monroar, Oscar Wildecat, Shaunberian White.

RABBIT

You're considered the luckiest (and cutest!) of the zodiac animals. Mothers in China want Rabbit babies almost as much as they want little Dragons (see below).

Lucky qualities: Kind. Compassionate. Sincere. Soft fur.

Unlucky qualities: Cautious. Conservative. Overly sentimental.

Lucky nail color: None. Don't even *think* of having your nails done. You've heard of a lucky rabbit's foot, haven't you? The less noticeable your paws are, the better.

Lucky hairstyle: Fluff and go! High-maintenance you are not.

Lucky careers: Carrot cake baker. Mesclun salad plater at a fancy restaurant for rich hares wearing harelooms.

Unlucky careers: Magician's assistant. Pet hair removal specialist.

Famous Rabbits: Carrotfucius, Albunny Einstein, Drew Bunnymore.

DRAGON

Dragon was the symbol of the emperor in ancient China. It is considered a great honor to be born under this sign. In China, more babies are born in Dragon years than any other.

Lucky qualities: Lively. Enthusiastic. Artistic. Gifted.

Unlucky qualities: You love to gossip. Perfectionist. Unrealistic expectations of others.

Lucky outfit for your date: Something flame-retardant.

Should you ask your crush out? Why not? No one says no to a dragon and lives to tell about it.

Lucky careers: Tortilla manufacturer. Murano glassblower. Deep fryer specialist. Prison guard.

Unlucky careers: Firefighter. Anger management coach. Gambler.

Famous Dragons: Scalevador Dalí, Sigmund Fireud, Puff Daddy.

SNAKE

The snake may be feared and shunned in Western culture, but in the East, it is a symbol of beauty and power. Snakes are viewed as mystical, deep-thinking, and mysterious.

Lucky qualities: Bookworm-ish. Wise. Charming. Soft-spoken. Strong intuition. You enjoy your own company.

Unlucky qualities: Procrastinator. Stingy. Vain.

Lucky stone: Granite. Perfect for sunning.

Lucky beauty product: Sunscreen.

Should you ask your crush out? Best to stay coiled. Pretend you're asleep, or don't care. Never chase, or you will lose them for sure! Once you have them, avoid wrapping and squeezing.

Lucky careers: Sunglasses model.

Unlucky careers: Snake-in-a-basket in Mumbai. NASCAR track maintenance specialist. Handbag.

Famous Snakes: Johannessss Brahmsssssss, Mahatmasssss Gandhissss, Jackie Onassissssss, Pablo Picassssssso.

HORSE

Horses have an amazing capacity for hard work. You enjoy traveling. You are your own person.

Lucky qualities: Independent. Friendly.

Unlucky qualities: Selfish. Cunning. Don't listen to advice.

Lucky nail color: Can do! Can do!

Lucky outfit for a date: You know you're always stylish. As famed fashion designer Coco Chaneigh once said, "Dress shabbily and they remember the dress; dress impeccably and they remember the horse."

Lucky school: Rode Island School of Design.

Unlucky career: Dental hygienist for gifted horses.

Famous Horses: Sir Issac Neighton, Marcus Trotllius Cicero, Jimi Horsedrix, Jackie Chanter.

SHEEP/GOAT/RAM

Sheep are prone to getting off on the wrong foot with others. But given a chance, you can be charming company.

Lucky qualities: Elegant. Creative. Emotional. Wanderer. Need a lot of time alone for imagining.

Unlucky qualities: Unorganized. High-strung. Pessimistic. Easily startled. Some are known for fainting when panicked.

Lucky scent: L'Air de Fainting Salts.

Lucky hairstyle: Random tufts. So cute!

Lucky crushes: Rabbit and Pig love you the way you are.

Unlucky crushes: Ox is not the dude but the dud for you.

Lucky career: Nightmare intervention counselor for children who ate too much sugar.

Unlucky sports: Synchronized swimming. Don't even try it.

Famous Goats: Leonardo da Vinsheep, Paul Goatguin, Winslow Herdmer, Baabaara Walters.

MONKEY

Monkeys are all about fun. You are well-liked and successful in any field you try.

Lucky qualities: Good at sharing. Upbeat. Witty.

Unlucky qualities: Drawn to danger. Easily discouraged.

Your best features: Toes! Tail is fun, too!

What not to wear on a date: (K)nits.

Unlucky crush: Tiger will play hard to get with you. Then Tiger will play easy to get. What a playful Tiger! Then suddenly . . . where is Monkey? Monkey?

Best first line for chatting up your crush: "Let's hang!"

What if your crush doesn't notice you? Monkeys are insecure about this and tend to overdo their attention-grabbing antics. Just breathe—not the death-rattle crescendo, but quiet like when you're on the monkey bars.

Lucky careers: Playground supervisor. Banana cultivation specialist in Ecuador.

Unlucky careers: Monkey's aunt. Monkey in the middle.

Famous monkeys: Chelsea Chimpton, Susan Banana Anthony, Charlesimian Dickens.

ROOSTER

Roosters tend to be arrogant, eccentric, and loud (or uncommunicative if you were born at night). You like to strut your stuff!

Lucky qualities: Lifelong learner. Hard worker. Decisive. You speak your own mind.

Unlucky qualities: A show-off. Dreamer. Flashy dresser.

Lucky hairstyle: Updo, as only you can.

Unlucky date outfit: Too many eggsessories.

Should you ask your crush out? Heck, yeah. As they say, the early bird catches the date!

Lucky careers: Class attendance monitor. Hotel wake-up call operator.

Unlucky careers: Underground mine carbon monoxide detector specialist. Red-eye flight pilot. Nightclub owner.

Famous Roosters: Cocktherine the Great, Henyard Kipling, Eggzra Pound.

DOG

The Dog will never let you down. Dogs born during the day tend to be docile. Dogs born at night, aggressive. Those born in between, passive-aggressive.

Lucky qualities: Loyal. Sensitive. Good secret keeper.

Unlucky qualities: Worrier. Dishonest. Self-righteous.

Lucky fashion choice: A blingy collar.

Unlucky fashion choice: Booties.

Should you chase that squirrel? Depends. Will your hair still look good afterward?

Unlucky crushes: Dragon. Secondhand smoke will kill you.

Lucky careers: Crime scene forensics expert. Queen-walker at Buckingham Palace.

Famous Dogs: Boltaire, Mutther Teresa, Madognna.

PIG

Pigs make splendid companions and lifelong friends. You have a very strong need to set difficult goals and carry them out.

Lucky qualities: Diplomatic. Sincere. Noble.

Unlucky qualities: Materialistic. Too trusting.

Lucky must-have car: Lamporkini. Cute cops will stop you just to get a closer look.

Lucky crushes: Rabbit and Sheep like the same movies you do, and will even laugh at the same lines.

Unlucky crushes: You're drawn to the cute bad-boy Monkeys. They'll hang around all day and crack you up with funny stories, but in the end, you'll find you'd rather be making mud dumplings than camping in the trees.

Lucky sports: Competitive ramen slurping. Competitive slurping anything.

Famous Pigs: The Dalai Salama, Hogry Ford, Ernest Hamingway, Luciano Pigvarotti, Hillary Rod*ham* Clinton.

Just remember, no matter what sign you're born under, you're in charge. Now go out there and lead your luckiest life!

BUT IT WAS REAL, BECAUSE EVERY TIME I WORE THE DRESS, SOMETHING BAD WOULD HAPPEN AND MY ☀ DAY WOULD CHANGE INTO ☁.

IF ENOUGH BAD THINGS HAPPEN YOU START TO NOTICE THEM.

IT MUST BE THIS DRESS.

IT'S BAD LUCK!

I'VE GOT TO GET HOME AND CHANGE BEFORE ANYTHING ELSE HAPPENS.

MUCH BETTER.

AND SAFER.

ONCE YOU DECIDE THAT SOMETHING IS BAD LUCK, THERE'S NO GOING BACK.

TODAY WOULD BE A PERFECT DAY TO WEAR MY DRESS.

IT'S SO CUTE!

AND I DO LOVE THE POCKES!

YES! WEAR ME!

WAIT, DO I LOVE BIRDS POOPING ON MY HEAD?

CARS SPLASHING ME WITH PUDDLES?

UNEXPLAINED SUDDEN DIARRHEA?

RAY OF SADNESS →

RAY OF GUILT ↑

RAYS OF RELIEF ↗

I'M SORRY DRESS, I CAN'T WEAR YOU AGAIN.

I'LL HAVE TO GIVE YOU AWAY.

THAT'S OKAY, SOME OTHER GIRL WILL LOVE YOU.

DEAR WORLD, I AM SORRY. PLEASE FORGIVE ME.

The World's Most Awkward Mermaid

By Sophie Blackall

When I was seven, my parents took us traveling for a month. I had a little suitcase with three outfits: three gingham shirts (red, green, and brown), three velour skirts (red, green, and brown) and three sweaters (red, green, and . . . well, I think you can see where this is going). I never once mixed and matched.

I have always been mad for a uniform.

When I was nine, I joined a bunch of sports teams just for the outfits, but once they realized I couldn't throw/catch/hit a ball I was dropped pretty quickly.

My elementary school did not have a uniform, but that didn't stop me from wearing one—or, actually, five. The week before fifth grade, my mother took me to a thrift store, and I picked out a different school uniform for every day of the week. They were all a bit baggy and had other girls' name tags sewn into the collars, and I imagined that those girls—Sally and Kirsty and Susie and Robyn and Ruth—were my long-legged older sisters. No one seemed to notice, or if they did, they asked, "Is that from your old school?" and I said, "Yep," even though I had been at the same school since kindergarten, usually with the kid who was asking the question.

In seventh grade, I went to an all-girls school, which was a drag, but I got to wear a uniform every day for real, which was excellent.

Except for the day I didn't, which wasn't.

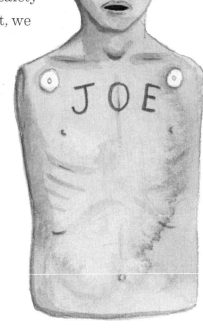

We all had to take swimming lessons, and, at the end, pass a water safety test. As part of the test, we each had to perform mouth-to-mouth resuscitation on a dummy, Joe, who was supposed to have water in his lungs. This was actually the least of Joe's problems, considering he didn't have any legs or arms.

Joe's rubber lips shone with my classmates' spit, and we had to pump his latex chest as though we meant it, or Miss Cox wouldn't pass us.

Nobody was too excited about that part.

However, *everyone* was excited about the next part. We each had to swim a length of the pool in our clothes so we'd know how to survive if we fell in accidentally, or had to jump in to save a drowning toddler. We weren't excited about swimming in our clothes; we were excited because we got to *change into clothes from home*.

Basically, this meant a fashion parade. Miss Cox had said, "Bring your oldest clothes," which we heard as "Bring your coolest clothes." Girls had been discussing what they were going to wear for weeks.

When the day came, my classmates filed out of the changing room in skinny jeans and leggings, in miniskirts and leg warmers.

I had gone in the other direction. I wore a 1950s circle skirt, which had yards and yards of fabric so if you twirled, it would spin way out. On top, I wore the coolest thing I owned: a fleece sweatshirt with batwing sleeves. Batwing sleeves are the kind that go from your wrist to your waist. I looked fabulous. I could flap and twirl like nobody's business.

Eighteen of us lined up at the end of the pool.

Miss Cox blew the whistle.

Eighteen of us jumped in.

Seventeen of us swam, laughing and screaming, to the other end.

One of us splashed and flapped her soggy batwings and began to twirl in desperation. To my horror, my now massively heavy, drenched circle skirt wrapped itself tightly about my legs, turning me into the world's most awkward mermaid.

I probably would have just sunk to the bottom of the pool, but Miss Cox made it a Teachable Moment, yanking me out by the wings and telling everyone how she saved my life.

I trudged home, dragging a plastic bag with my coolest clothes, a rumpled water safety certificate, and half the contents of the pool.

"Don't you want to change out of your uniform?" asked my mother.

I did not.

Now that I'm a grown-up, I can wear whatever I want, so I have invented my own uniform. Which is excellent. It is also streamlined, just in case.

Tell Your Future with Mad Libs®

Come! Learn your future the good old-fashioned way. With Mad Libs! We guarantee that these predictions will end up _____ percent true. Would we lie to you?
NUMBER

Job:

Well, there's no good way to put it. Your profession, when you grow up, is going to be _____. Yep. Just like
JOB
your dear old grandmama. There's no getting around it. But, good news! To make ends meet, you'll have *two* jobs, and that second job will be _____, like you
DIFFERENT JOB
always wanted.

Love:

One day you're in _____, _____ a particularly
PLACE   VERB ENDING IN "ING"
large _____, when you see a _____ by the name of ____
FOOD   GENDER   NAME

and BLAMMO! Love at first sight. Sure, it'll take a little

time to get used to how the love of your life likes to ___
BAD

_____ every five minutes, but believe me. It's worth it.
HABIT

Children:

Unfortunately for you, when it comes to their personal-

ities, your kids will resemble a mash-up of _____
WORST TEACHER

_____ and _____ and _____
IN YOUR SCHOOL   NASTIEST BULLY   LEAST FAVORITE

_____ . You'll have about _____ of them, too. And
SINGER   NUMBER

they'll all constantly talk like _____ .
LEAST FAVORITE CELEBRITY

All. The. Time.

Fame and Fortune:

Artist Andy Warhol once said that in the future every-

one will be famous for fifteen minutes. But you, my

friend, will be famous for _____ years. It's kind of a/an
NUMBER

_____ story. You see, while going out to pick up the
ADJECTIVE

_____ you were saving up for, you fall into a sinkhole full
NOUN

of _____ . _____ people record it while it happens, and
LIQUID   NUMBER

when a/an _____ , a/an _____ , and _____
          ANIMAL   **VEHICLE**   **YOUTUBE STAR**

also fall in, things start to get a little crazy. Thanks to

your smart thinking, you save everyone by stringing

your _____ and _____ together. The president
     PLURAL NOUN   **PLURAL NOUN**

later calls you the most _____ person in America.
                         ADJECTIVE

Death:

Thanks to the miracles of modern science, you might live

for another _____ years.
            NUMBER

Unless you don't, of course.

In the event that you clean your fingernails every day,

without fail, you'll live for _____ years
                             DIFFERENT NUMBER

instead. And that, ladies and gentlemen, is science!

My Life Being Funny (and How You Can Do It, Too)

By Adrianne Chalepah

Whether it's my impressive talent for tripping myself, or my ability to spill half my food in my lap, or because my face is, well, my face, I have always found a way to make people laugh—without really trying. Here's how I do it:

PERSISTENCE

I grew up in a small town on the Kiowa, Comanche, and Apache Indian reservation in Oklahoma, where most people were literally cowboys or Indians. And most Indians were cowboys. And most cowboys were Indians.

One beautiful spring day I was walking along and I saw a group of boys. One of them was cute and we weren't related. (*Score!*) I waved at him, and he smiled. His friends were whispering to him and pointing at me. *They're telling him, "Look, it's the smart, funny girl.*

That's a real woman. Go for it!" I thought to myself.

As I began to daydream about all the compliments I was undoubtedly getting, my neck whipped back and my body slammed to the ground. A sharp pain shot through my knee, and I looked down to see the culprit: a small rock. The only one for miles.

I looked up at my crush and his friends, who were doubled over in laughter. I smiled back and waved again. *I wonder if they'll come carry me to the doctor, like true gentlemen.*

Then they started to walk away from me. *I wonder if he'll still talk to me even though my knee is bleeding.*

I limped after the boys and said, "Hey, guys. How's it going?"

"Did you fall?" one boy asked.

"No."

"Yes, you did. We just saw you!"

"Oh. Well, why'd you ask? Hey, do you guys have a Band-Aid and maybe some antiseptic?"

They stared at me in silence.

"Okay. See you guys later!" I wobbled off, still smiling. *They're being shy because they like me so much,* I thought.

Lesson of the day: Have an unshakable sense of confidence. Even when you're literally bleeding.

* * *

INSPIRATION

I come from a family of storytellers, and I learned some of my best techniques from them. For example, I learned that some stories should never be told outside the home, or at least shouldn't be told in the presence of people who already think you're crazy. One of my uncles found this out for me.

My uncle Clint lived in the woods and spent a lot of time either hunting or fishing. He was also recently abandoned by his wife. Maybe that's why he spent a lot of time in the woods. I don't know.

One day Clint visited his doctor and told him a great story.

The story started off with Clint in the woods, go figure, alone. He was hunting for deer and stumbled upon a family of bigfoots.

"Excuse me. Did you say 'bigfoot,' Clint?" the doctor said.

"Yes, sir! And he was big and hairy, and he stunk like tha devil!"

"It was a male?" the doctor asked. "You sure?"

"Yes, sir, he was a male, and he had a baby bigfoot with him. But no momma bigfoot. Momma bigfoot was nowhere to be found."

After Clint told me this story, he added, "And now

I have to take some medicine so I don't see bigfoots no more."

Lesson of the day: Storytelling is great, but know your audience.

OBSERVATION

I am definitely a people-watcher. I study people, their accents, and what they eat. Mostly because I'm always hungry, but still.

My favorite person to watch is my mom. She's getting older, so she has to squint her eyes when she reads and she is easily confused. She talks to her computer like it can understand her.

"No. I do not want to take a survey. I want to pay my bill. Adrianne, can you get on the computer and pay my bill for me?"

I walk over to her desk and look at her screen.

"Mom, you already paid your bill. You're on a different site now, booking a vacation to the Bahamas."

"Shoot! How did I get here?"

"That's a good question."

Lesson of the day: Cherish these quirky moments with your parents. Learn to laugh instead of dying of shame and embarrassment. Then ask them if you can make fun of them in a published book. They love you, so they'll probably say yes. Besides, you help teach them about technology, so they owe you one.

POSITIVITY

Sometimes when I perform stand-up comedy, there are hecklers in the audience. This doesn't always go the way you'd expect.

A while back I did a show at a large casino in Arizona. A group of lively audience members was loudly chatting through my routine. But everything they said was . . . really nice.

"I think my husband is—"

"Oh no!" a woman in the audience called out. "Leave him, girl!"

"I'm trying to lose weight," I said, starting a new joke.

This time, a man in front yelled out, "You're beautiful!"

Are my hecklers encouraging me to have better self-esteem? Are these self-empowerment hecklers?

I was so confused by my positive hecklers that I almost didn't notice the one heckler who said, "You're not funny! Booo!"

Eventually that one negative guy was removed by security and I finished my show. Tempted to be saddened by his boos, I remembered instead the words of my supportive hecklers. I mean, yes, they seemed to have been drinking large amounts of alcohol, but they were right. I am beautiful.

Lesson of the day: Always listen to the positive hecklers and ignore the ones who boo.

About the Contributors

CECE BELL grew up in a very funny family. Her mom is particularly fond of potty humor. Her mom's mom was, too. Cece works in a barn in Virginia to make sure that her books are full of yuks. When she is not trying to figure out whether or not she should make an *El Deafo 2*, Cece hangs out with the funniest fella in the known universe, writer and illustrator Tom Angleberger. Cece and Tom sometimes make books together, like the Inspector Flytrap series (guaranteed to make you giggle). Check out Cece's books at cecebell.com.

SOPHIE BLACKALL is the illustrator of Ivy and Bean, The Witches of Benevento, and lots of picture books, including *Finding Winnie*, which won the 2016 Caldecott Medal. She grew up in Australia and went to an all-girls school, which was fine as long as you could make a joke and stay afloat. Literally. These days she shares a studio in Brooklyn with four boys who are all pretty funny, but don't tell them she said so.

LIBBA BRAY is the #1 *New York Times* bestselling author of *Beauty Queens, Going Bovine,* the Gemma Doyle Trilogy (*A Great and Terrible Beauty, Rebel Angels, The Sweet Far Thing*), and the Diviners series (*The Diviners, Lair of Dreams*). She once wore fake-mustache glasses to a funeral and an oversized, pink whoopee cushion costume to meet the head writer of *The Simpsons.* Both of these choices were major mistakes. You probably shouldn't have anything further to do with her, but if you insist, you can find her at libbabray.com. Just don't say we didn't warn you.

LISA BROWN is a *New York Times* bestselling illustrator, author, and cartoonist. Her books include *The Airport Book, Mummy Cat* by Marcus Ewert, *Emily's Blue Period* by Cathleen Daly, and *The Latke Who Couldn't Stop Screaming* by Lemony Snicket, to whom she is allegedly married. She lives in San Francisco but can most often be found wandering the Internet. Find her at americanchickens.com.

ADRIANNE CHALEPAH is a Native American (Kiowa/Apache) stand-up comedian, writer, and mother of three. She began performing on stage when she was nineteen years old, once gave the opening invocation for First Lady Michelle Obama, and formed the comedy group Ladies of Native Comedy.

ALISON DECAMP (*My Near-Death Adventures* (*99% True!*) and *My Near-Death Adventures: I Almost Died. Again.*) never met a book she hasn't liked. Unless it's scary. Or disturbing. Alison doesn't like to be scared. Or disturbed. When she was ten years old, Alison planned on playing professional football for the Pittsburgh Steelers and owning a deodorized skunk. When that didn't happen she became a teacher instead, which is practically the same thing. Alison lives and writes in northern Michigan with her kids and husband, none of whom find her very funny. They are wrong. You can find Alison at alisondecamp.com or (more likely) trapped under her very fat cat.

CARMEN AGRA DEEDY is the author of nine books for children, including *The Library Dragon*, *The Cheshire Cheese Cat*, *Martina the Beautiful Cockroach*, and *14 Cows for America*, a *New York Times* bestseller. Her personal stories first appeared on NPR's *All Things Considered*; funny, insightful, and frequently irreverent, Deedy's narratives are culled from her childhood as a Cuban refugee in the all-but-sleepy Southern town of Decatur, Georgia. A new picture book, *The Rooster Who*

Would Not Be Quiet (Scholastic Press) is scheduled for release in 2017. *The Book of Unintended Consequences* (Peachtree Publishers), a young adult novel, is scheduled for release in 2018.

KELLY DIPUCCHIO is the *New York Times* bestselling author of over twenty books for kids, including numerous humorous titles like *Everyone Loves Bacon*, *Gaston*, and *Zombie in Love*. Growing up, Kelly developed a sense of humor through adversity, like the time she threw up in gym class on the first day of seventh grade in a new school. "I didn't think anyone could survive that kind of public humiliation," she said, "but I learned to laugh about it and in the process I made a few new friends." Learn more about Kelly by visiting kellydipucchio.com.

MICHELLE GARCIA is the senior editor for race and identities at Vox.com, and a former editor at Mic.com and *The Advocate* magazine. Garcia studied journalism, political science, and women's studies at Oswego State University in New York, and screenwriting and producing at UCLA. She lives with her husband in Brooklyn.

LISA GRAFF is the author of numerous novels for young readers, including *A Tangle of Knots* (long-listed for the National Book Award), *Absolutely Almost* (an NCTE

Charlotte Huck Honor Book), *Lost in the Sun* (an ALA Notable Book), and most recently, *The Great Treehouse War.* A former children's book editor, Lisa now writes full time from her home outside of Philadelphia, where she lives with her family. You can learn more about Lisa and her books at lisagraff.com.

SHANNON HALE is the *New York Times* bestselling author of over twenty books for young readers, including *The Goose Girl*, the Ever After High trilogy, and Newbery Honor winner *Princess Academy.* With her husband, Dean Hale, she wrote the Princess in Black early chapter book series, the graphic novel *Rapunzel's Revenge*, and a novel about the Marvel superhero the Unbeatable Squirrel Girl. Her books for adults include *Austenland*, which was made into a very funny major motion picture. She is the mother of four children, including identical twin girls. In fact, most of what Henna and Greta say were things her four-year-old daughters actually said. So much of her story is true. If only it were also true that there are always more cookies.

CHARISE MERICLE HARPER has made many books for children. Sometimes she writes them, sometimes she draws them, and sometimes she does both. Her books include the Just Grace series, the Fashion Kitty series, and picture books such as *Cupcake, Go! Go!*

Go! Stop!, and *A Big Surprise for Little Card*. Charise likes to keep busy. New books for 2017 include *Mae and June and the Wonder Wheel*, The Amazing Crafty Cat (a new graphic novel series), and The Next Best Junior Chef (a new chapter book series). Charise loves books, but her favorite thing to do is to make comics.

JENNIFER L. HOLM AND MATTHEW HOLM are the sibling team behind the *New York Times* bestselling graphic novel *Sunny Side Up*. They are the creators of the Babymouse, Squish, My First Comics, and Little Babymouse series. The Eisner Award–winning Babymouse series has introduced millions of children to graphic novels. Jennifer is also the *New York Times* bestselling author of *The Fourteenth Goldfish* and several other highly acclaimed novels, including three Newbery Honor winners, *Our Only May Amelia*, *Penny from Heaven*, and *Turtle in Paradise*. Matthew is also the author, with Jonathan Follett, of the novel *Marvin and the Moths*.

AKILAH HUGHES is a writer, stand-up comedian, and YouTuber currently residing in Brooklyn. Her work has been viewed millions of times on Refinery29, Fusion, *The Huffington Post*, HelloGiggles, Femsplain, MTV, Yahoo!, and on her personal YouTube channel, *It's Akilah, Obviously!*. Visit her at itsakilahobviously.com.

AMY IGNATOW is the writer and illustrator of the Popularity Papers and the Mighty Odds series. She lives in Philadelphia with her family and seventeen rabbits, and often lies about having seventeen rabbits. She also hosts a bimonthly rabbit pageant featuring seventeen diverse and extraordinarily talented rabbits. Amy enjoys telling stories.

CHRISTINE MARI INZER has been drawing since she was old enough to hold a pencil in her hand. At the age of seventeen, she self-published her first book about her travels in Japan. Tuttle Publishing released a new edition of her book, a graphic novel entitled *Diary of a Tokyo Teen,* in 2016. Christine is currently a student at the University of Richmond and is looking forward to her next book. Visit her website at christinemari.com.

LENORE LOOK is the award-winning author of the popular Alvin Ho series and the Ruby Lu series, and several picture books, including *Brush of the Gods,* which was named a *Wall Street Journal* Best Children's Book of the Year. She was born a Tiger into a family of barnyard animals, which explains a lot of things. "Living with a wild animal in your barn is very exciting and a bit dangerous," she says. "It's a miracle I wasn't turned into a rug!" You can visit her on her blog at lenorelook. wordpress.com. She lives in Hoboken, New Jersey.

This is **MEGHAN MCCARTHY**'s first comic, but not her first strange and traumatic incident. In fact, Meghan has had so many strange and traumatic incidents that she could fill a library with her tales of woe. Is it because she goes looking for such events or because they are thrust upon her? Either way, Meghan isn't complaining (at the moment) because they give her much fodder to be shared with readers such as you. Visit her at meghan-mccarthy.com.

MITALI PERKINS has written several novels for young readers, including *Rickshaw Girl* (listed among the New York Public Library's 100 Great Children's Books, 100 Years) and *Bamboo People* (American Library Association's 2011 Best Fiction for Young Adults). She recently edited *Open Mic: Riffs on Life Between Cultures in Ten Voices*, an anthology exploring race and humor, and her newest novel, *Tiger Boy*, won the South Asia Book Award. Mitali was born in India and lived in Bangladesh, England, Mexico, Cameroon, and Ghana before acquiring her hyphen ("Indian-American") in the United States as a seven-year-old. She lives and writes in the San Francisco Bay Area.

LEILA SALES is the author of the YA novels *Tonight the Streets Are Ours*, *This Song Will Save Your Life*, *Past*

Perfect, and *Mostly Good Girls,* as well as the middle grade novel *Once Was a Time.* She has done improv and sketch comedy, helped judge the world's largest scavenger hunt, and given tours of a graveyard while wearing a Colonial gown, but her favorite hobby is sleeping. Visit her at leilasales.com.

RAINA TELGEMEIER is the #1 *New York Times* bestselling, multiple Eisner Award–winning creator of *Smile* and *Sisters,* which are both graphic memoirs based on her childhood. She is also the creator of *Drama,* which was named a Stonewall Honor Book and was selected for YALSA's Top Ten Great Graphic Novels for Teens. Raina lives in San Francisco, California. To learn more, visit her online at goraina.com. Her latest graphic novel is *Ghosts.*

DEBORAH UNDERWOOD is the author of numerous picture books, including *Good Night, Baddies; Interstellar Cinderella;* and *New York Times* bestsellers *The Quiet Book* and *Here Comes the Easter Cat.* Her feline companion, Bella, helped write Deborah's contribution to this book, although the real Bella wouldn't be caught dead living with a d-o-g. (When asked how she wrote so convincingly about a dog-loving cat, Bella tossed her head dramatically and replied, "I was *acting.*") Deborah and Bella live, write, and nap in Northern California.

URSULA VERNON is the award-winning author of the series Hamster Princess and Dragonbreath and the novel *Castle Hangnail*. She would like to be like her grandmother when she grows up. She writes, draws, and creates weird little things, and once nearly stepped on a rattlesnake. She currently lives in North Carolina with her husband, several cats, and a hound dog, and can usually be found wandering around the garden, trying to make eye contact with butterflies.

RITA WILLIAMS-GARCIA is the author of nine novels for young readers, including the multi-award-winning One Crazy Summer series featuring the Gaither sisters. She has been awarded the Newbery Honor and the Coretta Scott King Author Award for each book in the One Crazy Summer series, and has been twice named a National Book Award Finalist. Ms. Williams-Garcia is living her lifelong dream of training in the art of boxing at Gleason's Gym in Brooklyn, New York. She is the mother of two adult daughters, and she resides in Queens with her husband, Fred.

DELANEY YEAGER is a comedy writer and performer who won an Emmy for her work at *The Daily Show*, from 2014 to 2016. She began her television writing career on the Sundance show *The Approval Matrix*. Her play, *Waiting for AAA*, went to the 2015 NYC Fringe Fest. Before all of that that stuff, she was working as a hotel concierge. She graduated from Pace University's Performing Arts School in 2013.

MACKENZIE YEAGER is a writer on the *Boy Meets World* sequel *Girl Meets World* on Disney Channel. Before that, she worked on *The Haunted Hathaways* and *The Goldbergs*. She holds a BFA from The Theatre School at DePaul University and her plays have been produced in Los Angeles, New York, and Chicago. She also is a Liza Minnelli impersonator for the YouTube channel *Liza with a Vlog!*